Dear Reader,

In *Long Lost Husband*, I tried combining two of my favorite elements. The first is an exceptional love capable of surviving class differences, deception, tragedy and years of separation. The second element is mystery.

Whether it's Columbo's "Just one more question," Hercule Poirot's "little gray cells," Nick and Nora's tipsy antics, or the more hard-core adventures of Sam Spade, I have always been a sucker for a book or movie that presents me with a puzzle to be solved and an interesting man or woman to do the solving.

The idea for *Long Lost Husband* came as I was thumbing through a newspaper, and a "What if…?" puzzle popped into my mind. What if a woman sees what should be a stranger's photo in the newspaper and is convinced, despite all odds, that the man in the picture is her deceased husband? Then what if she confronts the man with her evidence, and he denies knowing her? And what if, while they debate the question, something evil closes in on them? Even better, I set the story in Texas, where I'd once lived for many years. It was the perfect place for my hero to remake himself.

I had a lot of fun solving my little mystery and bringing Andrea and Travis together in the process. I hope you have as much fun reading their story.

All the best,

Joleen Da

D0680845

GREATEST TEXAS LOVE STORIES OF ALL TIME

GREATEST
TEXAS LOVE STORIES
OF ALL TIME

LONG LOST HUSBAND
Joleen Daniels

Lone Star Lullabies

Silhouette® Books

Published by Silhouette Books
America's Publisher of Contemporary Romance

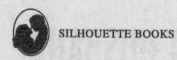 **SILHOUETTE BOOKS**

ISBN 0-373-65230-5

LONG LOST HUSBAND

Visit Silhouette at www.eHarlequin.com

Printed in U.S.A.

JOLEEN DANIELS

lives in Miami, Florida, where she tries to juggle a full-time job, a part-time writing career, an unmanageable husband and two demanding children. Her hobbies include housework and complaining to her friends.

Books by Joleen Daniels

Silhouette Romance

The Ideal Wife #891
Inheritance #939
Jilted! #990
Long Lost Husband #1043

Silhouette Special Edition

The Reckoning #507
Against All Odds #645

To Mr. Fred Schrager, the best "door" man I know;

And to Simone and Arthur Schimek—
may your life together be filled with love and happiness.

Prologue

Five years ago, her ex-husband had died. Five minutes ago, he'd suddenly come back to life.

Andrea Ballanger stared at the newspaper clipping on her desk and willed her hands to stop shaking. As a professor in the sociology department of a major Chicago university, objective analysis was second nature to her. Now she forced herself to ignore both the anger and the elation coursing through her and tried to bring that analytical ability to bear.

She'd been clearing her desk at the university in anticipation of taking the summer off to complete her thesis for her Ph.D. Under some books she'd found an old newspaper section that she had apparently left unread. She'd been about to discard it, when an article had caught her eye. A month-old account of the seemingly random shooting of a man and his pregnant wife in a San Antonio mall.

Her sensitivity to the senseless violence the article

detailed had been dulled by years spent watching the litany of horrors that passed as the nightly news. But the photo that accompanied this particular article would have touched a far more calloused heart than hers.

It was a close-up. A shattering picture of the aftermath of violence, of lives destroyed. A wounded private detective by the name of Travis Hunter cradling his unconscious wife in his arms on the floor of a shopping mall concourse in Texas. The rage, the anguish reflected on his features had called up an answering anger and sorrow in Andrea.

Reluctantly, unwillingly, she had studied the face of the wounded man as memories of her own policeman ex-husband's violent death in an ambush of gunfire coursed through her. For a moment, the two faces had overlapped in her mind: Travis Hunter, Trey Morgan. When her vision had finally cleared, a chill had run up her spine. It hadn't been her imagination. Travis Hunter bore an uncanny resemblance to her own dead ex-husband, Trey.

And now, no matter how carefully she studied the photograph, that resemblance still remained. But she had to be mistaken. After all, Trey had been dead for five years. Inevitably, her memory of his features had been blurred by the passage of time. The differences between the two men would become apparent once she compared an actual photograph of Trey to the one from the newspaper.

Her heart pounding, she reached into her purse and pulled out her wallet. Locating the section of plastic-covered photos, she turned unerringly to the one at the back. It was a photo that Trey had taken for his police academy graduation.

Placing the photos next to each other, she compared the two faces feature by feature. The resemblance between Travis Hunter and Trey Morgan seemed even stronger.

Andrea sat staring into space, remembering the events of five years ago. She had left Trey after two years of marriage and filed for divorce at a time when she was physically and emotionally devastated. Trey had gone to her lawyer's office and signed the divorce papers without even trying to contact her for an explanation. And he had been killed only days after the divorce had become final.

Now she was a woman with a job she loved, enough family wealth to last a lifetime, and a position in Chicago society that many woman would have killed to attain. The one thing she didn't have was peace of mind.

In the five years since the shooting, she had compared every man she'd dated to Trey, and they had all suffered from the comparison. She'd lain awake at night plagued by guilt and second thoughts, wishing she could have just one more chance to talk to Trey about what had happened, to try to figure out why things had gone so wrong between them. One more chance to resolve their relationship so that she could get on with her life.

This Travis Hunter couldn't be Trey. She knew that. But what if—*just suppose*—he was? Maybe she'd been given the second chance she'd prayed for so often. Now what was she going to do with it?

She was a person who valued self-control, someone who never did anything she hadn't carefully considered beforehand. She would have sworn that her logical nature would have prevented her from acting on impulse—especially given such flimsy evidence. Yet her hand reached for the phone.

"I'd like to make a reservation for your earliest available flight to San Antonio. Yes, I'll hold."

She would go to San Antonio and confront this Travis Hunter face-to-face. If by some miracle he was Trey Morgan, she promised herself she would learn the truth about the past. Then, and only then, would she finally be free.

Chapter One

"I'm not the man you were married to, lady. That man is as dead as my wife is! Now get out of here and leave me alone."

Her cheeks flushed in reaction to his shouted denial, Andrea met the glare of the large, angry man reclining in the hospital bed. Everything in her demanded that she retreat with as much dignity as she could salvage. But she couldn't bring herself to leave. Not yet. Not until she was sure that this man, a private detective who called himself Travis Hunter, wasn't Trey Morgan, the Chicago policeman she'd married seven years ago.

She forced herself to ignore both Travis Hunter's anger and the emotions coursing through her own being, and tried to look at the evidence objectively.

The man facing her was telling at least part of the truth. The woman he had called his wife, Lissa Jackson Hunter, had been killed about a month before. It was that death, or rather the newspaper article that had reported Lissa Hunter's shooting, that was responsible for bringing Andrea to this hospital room in San Antonio.

To her surprise, once she'd flown to San Antonio, she'd had to resort to the social connections she usually disdained in order to even locate Travis Hunter. A call to the governor of Illinois, a frequent guest at her mother's many parties, had produced rapid results. Within hours, Andrea had found the man she'd been looking for in a San Antonio hospital—despite the fact that he was not on the official roster of patients.

Now she had finally confronted Travis Hunter, and he'd barely given her a chance to explain her presence before he'd shouted out his denial.

"Are you deaf, lady? Or just crazy? I told you to leave!"

Andrea felt more blood rush to her face in response to his derisive tone. But even she had to admit that, to an objective observer, she might seem foolish, if not deranged. On the strength of a superficial resemblance she had flown hundreds of miles and had intruded on a man who was mourning the death of a loved one. A man who was still in the process of healing, emotionally as well as physically.

If he was who he claimed to be, a stranger, then he had every right to be angry. If he wasn't...

She had to know the truth.

"I've come a long way, Mr. Hunter," she said softly, cajolingly. "I realize I'm intruding. But since I'm already here, surely you could grant me a few more minutes of your time."

Without waiting for a reply, she stepped closer to the bed.

Travis Hunter grabbed the one bed rail that was elevated, and hauled himself up into a sitting position. "Hold it right there, or I'll call Mike in here and have you thrown out!"

Andrea hesitated. She had already met Mike Manelli, the guard at the hospital room door, on her way in. Manelli, one of the investigators employed by Travis Hunter's detective agency, had obviously been intrigued by her story—and by her appearance, as well, if the frankly admiring gleam in his dark eyes had been any indication. She had charmed him into granting her a five-minute audience with his boss, but she had no doubt that he would drag her from the room without hesitation if his employer summoned him and gave the order. She couldn't allow that to happen. Not yet.

"Why are you so anxious to get rid of me, Mr. Hunter? Do you have something to hide?" she asked, stalling for time, inching closer, counting the steps that would bring her to his side.

"I have better things to do than waste time talking to someone like you." His gaze flicked over her disdainfully. "Real pearl necklace, designer suit, Gucci leather. Impeccable style, impeccable background, impeccable breeding. Why don't you go organize some fund-raiser for the less fortunate and leave me the hell alone?"

The intended insult stung Andrea. She had learned long ago that, to most people, what she had and who she was related to would always be more important than who she was inside. It was a fact of life she had never quite been able to accept. Even Trey had resented the wealth and social status she'd been born with.

She forced a smile as she continued to ease forward. "Strange that you'd say that, Mr. Hunter. My ex-husband used to feel exactly the same way about my money and my family. Sort of reverse snobbery."

Holding his suddenly narrowed gaze, that glare that gave away nothing but hostility, she approached him with all the respect and caution of a wild-animal trainer attempting to keep a snarling tiger at bay, knowing that only her belief in her own ability to control him stood between her and disaster.

Silently, she willed him to accept her challenge, praying that his pride wouldn't let him call for help. Praying that he would give her the time she needed to discover the truth.

She came to a halt a foot away from him, close enough to touch, but not daring to. Close enough to almost feel the negative emotions that emanated from him. Ignoring his anger and her own apprehension, she examined him feature by feature.

He seemed to be about the right height—though it was hard to tell with him lying down. She was tall herself, but at six foot four Trey had towered over her, as husky and muscular as any linebacker on the pro teams whose games he'd watched so religiously. This man was big and muscular, but his face was too thin. She felt that if it were not for the covering of his hospital gown, she would have been able to see the outline of his ribs. Then again, he *had* been in the hospital for over a month, recovering from the near-fatal bullet wounds he'd received in the shopping mall.

Blocking that image from her mind, she let her gaze trail slowly upward. The width of his shoulders seemed right, but it had been so long since the last time she'd held her ex-husband in her arms. So long…

"Are you through with your *inspection?*"

Summoned by his growled question, her gaze snapped back to his. An unexpected wave of sensual awareness skittered across her nerve endings, but she hid her discomfort in a reply that was as brusque as his question. "Not quite."

Fighting for an objectivity that was usually second nature to her, she continued her examination. His eyes were the correct shade of blue, but then a lot of men had eyes that color. His voice was lower and raspier, the line of his jaw slightly more pronounced. But her ex-husband, Trey, had been "killed" by bullet wounds to the face and throat. He would have needed extensive plastic surgery if he had survived. Travis's closely trimmed beard could be hiding the scars.

His coal black hair seemed to be the right color, but Travis's curled down over his neck while Trey's had always been neatly trimmed.

She longed to touch it, as if she could discover the truth by touch alone. But the look in his eyes told her he'd read her intent and warned her that he wouldn't tolerate a further invasion of his privacy.

Restraining herself, fighting for control, Andrea tallied up the points. Different voice, different jawline, and all the features Travis did have in common with Trey could be explained away as superficial, coincidental. She still had no facts to back her up, only assumptions.

And even if by some wild, improbable twist of fate this man was Trey, he had denied it, and her. It was clearly time to leave, to bow out gracefully while she still had a shred of self-respect left to cling to.

But, somehow, she couldn't seem to take a step toward the door. Details of her ex-husband's appearance had been blurred by the passing years, but the feelings he had aroused in her were as fresh as if it had all happened yesterday. Logic be damned. She *knew* that this man was Trey Morgan. She knew because of the way he had made her feel from the second she'd entered the hospital room. The piercing stare that could cut her heart to ribbons between one breath and the next was as familiar to her as her own heartbeat. The emotional reaction he'd drawn from her with just a few angry words. The current of sensual awareness that she'd never felt with any other man.

Tears stung the backs of her eyes. "Why are you lying to me, Trey?"

He looked up at her, his face impassive, his eyes revealing nothing. "How many times do I have to say it before it sinks in? I'm not Trey Morgan!"

"Prove it." The words were delivered in an even, controlled tone, but Andrea was not in control of her feelings. Inwardly, she was a seething mass of pain and resentment. She longed to walk out the door and forget she'd ever seen this man. Why was she putting herself through this? Whoever he was, he'd made it very plain that he no longer wanted her in his life. And hadn't that been true of Trey even before he'd been gunned down in that back alley? The love between her ex-husband and herself had died long ago. So there was no reason that she should care, one way or the other. But she did care, profoundly. She cared about the truth.

It was the truth she had come to San Antonio to find, not her ex-husband. She had a right to that truth. She had a right to resolve all the old feelings that had been called up by the newspaper photograph, to finally end a relationship she had never been able to truly bring to a close. She had to do that or she would never be able to get on with her life.

"Prove it?" he echoed, his lip curling up on one side in a scornful expression that was eerily familiar. "How am I supposed to prove that I'm not who you think I am?"

"It's very simple. Trey had a knife scar on his left shoulder, a souvenir from a criminal who resisted arrest. All you have to do is show me that it's not on your shoulder and you'll never see me again."

"I think I've put up with this nonsense long enough. Get out and get out now, or I'll have you dragged out."

Andrea knew he was serious, knew that she had pushed him as far as she could. But she couldn't stop now.

"If that's the way you feel…" She half turned away, away from him, toward the door. Then she twisted back, trying to catch him off guard. Her hand snagged the loose, untied neck of the hospital gown and pulled downward.

But even as her fingers closed around the pale blue

material, his fingers closed around her wrist, yanking her toward him with a strength that, unleashed, could easily have snapped bone.

As it was, he was applying just enough pressure to numb her fingers, to force her to release her grip on the gown. Lying half across him, she hung on to the garment with a determination fully as strong as the rock-hard muscles in his hand.

"Let go, dammit," he said through clenched teeth, his jaw set. "I don't want to hurt you."

"Then *you* let go."

Andrea was breathing heavily, straining against his hold as if they were in an arm-wrestling match where the stakes were life or death. A long strand of brunette hair came loose from the severely elegant twist she favored and pooled on the thin cotton that still covered his chest. A bead of sweat ran down her temple as a remote, detached part of her brain wondered what her mother would say if she could see her debutante daughter now. Andrea knew beyond a doubt that the older woman would be scandalized. At the moment, she could have cared less.

The outside world had ceased to exist. There was only the unrelenting pressure on her wrist, the labored sound of her breathing, the heat and hardness of his body under hers.

Their gazes locked, ice blue with gold-flecked brown, so close that no other features were discernible. And, suddenly, Andrea found herself gazing directly into Trey Morgan's eyes. The last sliver of doubt vanished and she was hurtled back in time by the sight, the smell, the feel of a man she thought she'd lost forever.

She could feel the pressure of his chest against her breasts, the incredible heat of his body reaching her even through the layers of material she wore. She could feel his arousal pressing against her hip. But she felt no embarrassment. The sensual electricity flowing between them was so familiar it felt like coming home. Coming home after years spent wandering in a cold, lonely world that had no Trey Morgan to warm it and give it life.

Abruptly, his hand left her wrist to wrap around her nape, exploring, caressing, exerting a pressure that urged her ever closer.

With a moan of longing, Andrea cast aside her questions and her doubts. Closing her eyes, she gave in to the pressure, seeking a solace she had longed for through years of emptiness.

His lips took hers with a longing that matched her own, his tongue deepened the possession, melding with hers in a hot, wet completion that shook her to her soul.

She sank deeper and deeper into the kiss until she thought she would be lost forever. Then, suddenly, her conscious mind reasserted itself. This man had made her miserable while they were married. He'd disappeared from her life years ago, letting her believe that he was dead. And now that she'd found him, he'd insulted and rejected her. What was she doing melting in his arms like some brainless floozy?

She let go of the hospital gown, twisting her mouth away from his, pushing against his chest. Abruptly, he released her. She stumbled backward, fighting to regain her balance.

Free from the spell of his nearness, she blinked rapidly, trying to get her bearings, trying to absorb what had just happened. "Why...why did you do that?" she sputtered.

For a moment, she could have sworn that he looked as confused as she felt. Then a look that was plain disgust crossed his features.

"It's very simple, ma'am. Brute force didn't seem to be doing the job, so I figured a little sexual harassment might get you to back off. I'd say it worked."

Andrea felt the blood rush to her face as she absorbed what he'd said. But before she could even begin to find the words to express her outrage, there was a tapping sound on the hospital room door and it was pushed open.

A short, plump, bespectacled young woman appeared in the opening and gave them both a tentative smile. "Remember me, Mr. Hunter? I'm Janice Murphy, the social worker. Did the nurse tell you I'd be coming down to see you?"

Travis shifted the bedcovers and ran a hand over his mouth, eliminating the traces of lipstick that Andrea had left behind. "Yeah...uh, she did tell me about it."

Andrea's hand went to her own mouth, then to her hair. She hurriedly pushed the stray strand back into place and gathered the threads of her scattered dignity. Head high, she moved toward the door. "I'll wait outside."

The social worker glanced from one to the other, obviously sensing she was intruding. "Please, don't

let me interrupt. This will only take a minute. I just
need your signature on these papers, Mr. Hunter. The
ones giving your friends, Rob and Jenny Emory, per-
mission to remove your baby from the hospital.''

Andrea froze in place, a cold feeling of shock coursing through her. A baby? Then she remembered that
Lissa Hunter had been pregnant when the shooting had
occurred. The baby had survived!

Despite the way Trey—or Travis, or whatever this
man chose to call himself—had treated her, she was
glad for him. She pushed aside the feelings of envy
and sadness that threatened to engulf her, the endless
litany of how different her life would have been ''if
only,'' and made herself concentrate on the present.

Travis signed the papers and handed them and the
pen back to Ms. Murphy. The social worker hesitated
for a moment as if unsure whether to broach the subject. ''Would you like to come down to the nursery
and see Bonnie, Mr. Hunter?''

Travis looked up at her with a frown. ''Bonnie?''

Andrea could have sworn that the other woman
blushed. ''Oh…well, I realize that your little girl
hasn't actually been named yet. But the nurses have
taken to calling her Bonnie because she's the prettiest
baby in the nursery. I guess I picked it up from them.
I hope you don't mind.''

''The name's fine with me,'' Travis said, his voice
as emotionless as if he were discussing the weather.
''But about visiting the nursery, I just don't feel up to
it today. Maybe some other time.''

The social worker shifted her feet, glancing at Andrea as if trying to enlist her support. ''I know these

circumstances aren't ideal—Bonnie over her respiratory problems and finally ready to go home and your needing to stay on in the hospital. But there's a class you can attend while you're here that will teach you everything you need to know about taking care of a baby. That way, when you do take over Bonnie's care—''

Travis interrupted her monologue, not quite making eye contact. ''Thanks. I'll let you know.''

''Oh. Well, if you want to talk to me, just tell one of the nurses.'' With a final smile at Andrea, the woman left the room.

Andrea looked at Travis speculatively. ''You aren't going to take over the baby's care at all, are you?''

Travis turned his head toward her, his glance as hard and cold as it had been before their kiss. ''*That* is definitely none of your business. As to your other claim…''

Slowly, deliberately, he pulled down the neck of his hospital gown to expose the thick, white bandage covering his left shoulder. He spoke with a quiet finality that was more intimidating than a raised voice could ever be. ''There was a knife scar there once, Andrea, but it's gone now. Just like that man who loved you is gone. Trey Morgan died a long time ago, and there's nothing you can say or do that will ever bring him back to life.''

She watched as he closed his eyes and turned his face toward the wall. Still shaken by the emotions and memories that had been aroused by the kiss, she felt the shock of his dismissal like a slap in the face. He was as good as admitting that he had been Trey Morgan, that he had been her husband. But now he felt she wasn't even entitled to as much as an explanation of why he had faked his death and disappeared.

Andrea opened her mouth to rant at him, to tell him what she truly thought of him. But to her shame, she felt her throat swell with emotion and she knew that if she didn't leave the room, the next sound that would come out of her mouth would be a sob. And she wasn't going to give this man the satisfaction of seeing her cry. She needed time alone, time to think.

Andrea pulled open the door of the room and rushed into the hallway, almost colliding with a surprised Mike Manelli. She strode past him and down the corridor toward the elevator, her heels *rat-a-tat-tatting* on the linoleum.

Pushing open the door of the ladies' room, she slid inside. Thank God she was the only occupant! She leaned over the first sink she came to, gripping a side with each hand.

In the mirror above the sink she saw a woman whose cheeks were flushed with anger and whose eyes were deep wells of hurt. But beneath her anger there was a growing apprehension. She had told herself that she was coming to see this man because she had a right to know the truth of what had happened five years ago. She hadn't counted on the fact that this Travis Hunter would arouse a desire in her that she'd thought long dead. Or was *love* a better word?

Determinedly, she shook that thought off. The love she had felt for Trey Morgan had ended long ago. She had been a different person then. What she had felt just now was sexual attraction, nothing more. Sex had always been good between her and Trey. It had been the only time she could forget herself and let go completely. But that hadn't saved her marriage.

Closing her eyes, she let her head hang, trying to think, willing the emotional storm to pass.

If that man was Trey Morgan—and she knew he was—then he had played dead and changed identities for a reason. Had he been forced to take on a new identity to protect himself after the shooting in Chicago five years ago? Or had that whole shooting been a hoax? And what about the shooting that had happened a month ago in the San Antonio mall?

When the governor had called back to tell her where to find Travis Hunter, he had also warned her against revealing that information to anyone else. He had said that all the secrecy was just a precaution since the gunman from the San Antonio shooting hadn't been caught yet. Travis's posting a guard at the hospital door could be for the same reason.

Maybe that was the truth as far as it went, but maybe something more complex was happening here.

Her mind whirling, she gave up trying to solve the puzzle. Travis Hunter—to preserve her sanity, she resolved to try to think of him only by that name from now on—was the man with all the answers. And she wasn't going to leave him alone until he shared them with her. He owed her that much. She would go back to his room and tell him so. But first she would go to the hospital cafeteria and have a cold drink. When she felt able to discuss things in a rational manner, that would be the time to confront him.

After repairing her hair and makeup, Andrea left the

rest room and headed toward the elevator. She had just pressed the call button when she heard footsteps behind her.

"Are you a friend of Mr. Hunter's?"

Andrea turned in the direction of the question and looked straight into Janice Murphy's myopic brown eyes. In no mood for a long explanation or a discussion of a situation even she didn't fully understand, Andrea responded with a streamlined version of the truth. "I'm Andrea Ballanger from Chicago. My family is related to Travis Hunter's by marriage."

Thankfully, the social worker didn't ask for any details. "We all feel sorry for Mr. Hunter. Talk about a tragedy! The baby was born prematurely due to the shooting, and the mother only lived for a few minutes afterward."

Ms. Murphy shook her head and sighed. "And for a while, we thought we'd lose the father, too. You know he seemed more responsive today than he has been in the last month."

"Really?" Andrea said, her anger fading a bit as she wondered about the significance of that piece of information.

"I was hoping that he'd finally agree to see his little girl."

"He hasn't seen her at all?" Andrea asked, frowning, sure that she'd misunderstood. "Not even once?"

The elevator bell sounded, and Ms. Murphy sighed again as she watched the doors slide open. "Well, poor Bonnie didn't come into the world under the best of circumstances, that's for sure. In view of what happened, counseling really is indicated, but so far Mr.

Hunter has refused to discuss it. It's a shame. There are so many childless couples who would give anything to have a baby like Bonnie to lavish love and attention on.''

Andrea looked away, swallowing the bitterness and pain the other woman's words had unwittingly called up. If anyone could testify to the truth of that statement, she could. ''You're right, I'm sure.''

The social worker stepped into the empty car, then turned to face Andrea. ''Going up?''

''What?'' Andrea pulled her thoughts away from the gloom of the past and focused on Ms. Murphy. ''Oh, no, I'm going down to the cafeteria.''

''Well, then, it was nice meeting you, Ms. Ballanger.''

''Andrea.''

''Andrea. Have a safe trip home.''

Andrea watched the elevator doors closing, the anger she had felt earlier fading into melancholy. When she finally found out the truth of what had happened five years ago would her life be any different? Or would it still be just as empty emotionally as it was now? She was afraid she already knew the answer to that question, and it haunted her.

A frown creased her forehead as she saw Ms. Murphy's hands slip into the small space that remained between the elevator doors to prevent them from closing. ''Andrea, I'm on my way up to the nursery now. Do you want to come with me and see Bonnie? Come on, hurry!''

Andrea hesitated, trying to think. But there wasn't time to think. She opened her mouth to refuse and instead found herself squeezing aboard the elevator. The doors whisked shut behind her, and she was trapped.

A feeling of panic gathered in the pit of her stomach as the elevator began its ascent. What was she doing? The scene with that man must have addled her brain!

For five years she had done her best to avoid baby showers, christenings, anything and any place that might remind her. Now here she was volunteering to go see a baby. Trey's—Travis's—baby.

Desperately, she tried to formulate an excuse, a reason she could give the social worker for staying aboard the elevator. But, suddenly, her mind was a blank. Before she knew it, they had reached their destination.

The elevator came to a stop, the doors opened, and Ms. Murphy alighted. She began walking down the hall, obviously assuming that Andrea would follow.

Andrea stood poised on the threshold, unsure what her next move would be. Even from here she could hear muffled crying. The sound cut through her like a knife. What was she going to do now? And why, oh why, had she come this far? All at once, the answer came to her. This was Trey's baby, and she couldn't leave without seeing her. If she did, she'd wonder about her for the rest of her life.

Taking a deep breath, she forced herself out of the elevator and hurried to catch up with her guide. They turned a corner together, and there it was. The glass observation window of the nursery and row after row of newborns.

The old familiar pain lanced through Andrea, the regret, the anger, and most of all the hunger. The hun-

ger that never truly went away. She pressed her lips
together, willing herself to maintain control, telling
herself that she could get through this.

And then Ms. Murphy was taking her by the arm
and leading her forward. "Oh, it's time for her feeding! Would you like to?" She rapped lightly on the
glass. "Look who I brought you, Linda. Someone
from little Bonnie's family!"

What happened next Andrea watched in a curiously
detached way. She entered a small room near the nursery and a nurse moved forward to slip a gown over
Andrea's suit. Both the nurse and the social worker
chattered animatedly, as excited as if they had a per-
sonal stake in Bonnie Hunter's future. Vaguely, Andrea realized that they did. Obviously, they cared for
the baby and very much wanted Bonnie to have loving
relatives who shared that affection. And all she was
doing was satisfying her idle curiosity.

The numbness disappeared and guilt suffused her.
She wanted to run away, to go home to Chicago where
she could pretend that this whole futile trip had been
just a bad dream. But it was too late. She was already
sitting in a rocking chair, and a bundle of softness and
warmth was being thrust into her arms. Instinctively,
she closed her arms around it. She found herself looking down at a tiny, round face whose solemn blue eyes
seemed to be regarding her assessingly. With a shock,
she realized that she had seen those very same eyes
only moments before in a much bigger, much more
hostile face.

She was holding Trey's baby. The child of a man

who had denied and rejected her. Just as he seemed to be rejecting this daughter of his.

But suddenly, none of that mattered. A tiny hand reached out and latched on to her finger with a determined grip, and the hunger that had burned in Andrea for five long years was finally stilled. She looked down at the baby with a kind of awe, tears shining in her eyes.

"Hello, Bonnie," she whispered.

The baby gurgled in response, and Andrea's heart, the heart that had always assumed that motherhood was based on blood ties, dropped its guard and welcomed a stranger home.

The man who called himself Travis Hunter sat in his hospital bed praying that the drifting numbness of the last month would return to claim him. But he already knew the prayer was futile. The protective apathy was gone for good. In its place was a soul-deep agony that threatened to rob him of his sanity.

Because of him, Lissa was dead. She'd been so full of life that it was hard to believe she was gone. They had never been wildly in love—he'd stopped believing in romantic love long ago—but she had made him laugh, something it seemed he hadn't done for years. When she'd found out she was pregnant, he'd gladly agreed to marry her. The idea of a wife like Lissa and a baby on the way had given him something to look forward to, something to wake up for each morning. Now, there was only emptiness.

With a moan of mental and physical anguish, Travis threw the covers aside and let his feet slide to the floor.

Since regaining consciousness in this hospital a month before, he had fought with all his strength to feel nothing, to keep the memory of Lissa's death at bay until he was strong enough to take the action that he had planned. But he hadn't anticipated Andrea's visit. She had awakened him from his self-imposed emotional coma.

When he'd seen her come into the room, he hadn't been able to believe his eyes. His first feeling had been one of righteous rage. Five years ago, just when he'd needed her the most, she'd turned her back on him. Now she had the gall to come charging into his life again because she'd seen some newspaper photo. Well, he didn't owe her anything, least of all an explanation. He wanted nothing from her, not even memories.

Unbidden, the kiss they'd just shared rose up to nag at him like a half-finished thought. He had done it to prove that he was free of Andrea, emotionally as well as physically, to prove he no longer cared. It had ended up scaring the hell out of him because he *had* felt something. Something he had never felt with Lissa or any other woman.

His hand shaking slightly, he ignored the pain in his chest and poured himself a glass of water from the plastic pitcher on the bedside table. The self-disgust he'd felt after Andrea had broken free of his embrace returned, and his lips formed a hard, thin line of denial. Sure he'd felt something when he'd touched her—the same unbelievable sexual chemistry that had always flashed between them. Bed had been the only place they'd ever understood each other's needs.

Cool, quiet Andrea. Andrea, who never raised her voice. Who, when he'd raised his, had retreated into a wounded, dignified silence that was as unbreachable as any fortress. Andrea, who had left him with that silence still unbroken, without a word of either explanation or regret.

He drained the glass in two swallows and set it back on the table. Despite his pain, he almost smiled. Had that steel-spined hoyden trying to rip off his hospital gown really been Andrea Ballanger, of the Chicago Ballangers? Maybe the years had changed her, after all. Maybe he should have talked to her, should have explained....

He shook off that disturbing urge and pushed away the bedside table. Second thoughts were a waste of time. She was on her way back to Chicago by now, and that was just as well. One woman was already dead because of him. He wasn't going to put anyone else at risk. Not Andrea, and certainly not the baby.

For one unguarded moment, he let his thoughts drift to the crib he'd put together, the room he'd painted, the plans that he and Lissa had had for the future. But those plans had died with his wife. The baby was better off with Jenny and Rob. They would love her and give her a good life. He had nothing left to give, to her or to anyone.

With grim determination, he pushed off of the bed and stood upright. A wave of weakness flashed through him, and, for a second, he was afraid his legs would refuse to hold him. Then the weakness passed. Slowly and carefully, he made his way to the closet and took out the fresh set of clothes that one of the employees of his security and investigations agency had had the foresight to bring in for him. Letting the hospital gown drop to the floor, he began to dress.

"What the hell are you doing?"

Travis turned his head and saw Mike Manelli gaping at him from the doorway. "What does it look like I'm doing? Come in and shut the door, you're letting in a draft."

He pulled on his slacks and zipped them up as Mike obeyed his instructions. "I want you to find out what kind of release I have to sign to spring myself from this joint and get it to me."

"But the doctor said you had to stay here for at least two more weeks."

"I don't care what the doctor said. I'm the one who's paying your salary. Now move!"

Mike crossed his arms over his chest and leaned back against the door, obviously unimpressed by his boss's surliness. "Was that a threat?"

Travis didn't even spare his right-hand man a glance as he finished buttoning his shirt. "It sure as hell sounded like one to me," he said evenly.

"This wouldn't have anything to do with that lady who came to see you earlier, would it?"

Deciding that socks just weren't worth the effort, Travis slid his feet into his shoes. *Lady.* Not woman or girl. Lady. That's what Andrea had always been, all right. It was an aura that surrounded her like that expensive perfume she still wore.

She'd made it clear that she was through with him even before his "death." What had made her come looking for him now? He would have liked to have the answer to that question. But he'd done the right thing. It wouldn't have done either of them any good to dredge up a past that had been buried with Trey Morgan. Especially since Travis Hunter only had a few weeks of future left.

Pulling his thoughts back to the subject at hand, he looked at Mike and shrugged. "I guess in a way, my leaving the hospital does have something to do with my visitor. If she could find me here, someone else might be able to do the same."

Mike straightened up abruptly. "You still need those two weeks to recuperate before you'll be good for anything. Where are we going to hide out?"

"You mean where am *I* going to hide out."

"You've got to be kidding! Why—"

Travis continued, talking over Mike's protest. "Because I'm the boss. And because it's less conspicuous if I go alone, and less conspicuous means safer. I want you to go back to the office and tell anyone who calls or comes in that I've gone out of the country to finish recuperating. England sounds good."

"Okay, *boss,* but where are you really going?"

"Lissa…" He hesitated, the sound of his dead wife's name rubbing him raw. "Lissa owned a house in a little town west of here called Layton City."

Mike shook his head. "Never heard of it."

"Neither has anyone else. Lissa and I have lived here in San Antonio ever since we got married. It's highly unlikely that anyone could trace me to Layton City or that house."

"And if by some chance they do?"

Travis finished pulling his shoulder holster into

place and shoved a clip into his gun. He looked at Mike with a gaze as cold as death. "Then I guarantee you that when they find me, they'll wish they hadn't bothered."

"If you come back tomorrow about the same time, you can feed her again. That is, if you want to."

Andrea smiled at the nurse as she stepped out into the corridor. "Oh, I want to."

She lingered outside the nursery window, watching possessively as the baby was placed back into her crib. Giving Bonnie back to the nurse had been like giving away some vital part of herself. She had been able to endure it because she'd convinced herself that the separation would only be temporary. She had to believe that, or she'd go mad.

She started for the elevator, part of her happier than she'd ever been, another part of her near despair. What had she done? How could she have allowed herself to form a bond with—to literally fall in love with—someone else's baby? But then, she hadn't *allowed* anything. Somehow, it had just happened.

All her life, she'd looked down on people who used that tired excuse to justify their actions. Things didn't just happen to Andrea Ballanger. She was much too sensible for that. She planned for every contingency. At least she had until today. Today, she didn't recognize herself. Her actions were suddenly being governed by emotions and impulses that were confusing and more than a little frightening.

No, they weren't frightening. They were terrifying.

Boarding the elevator, she pressed the button that

would take her to Travis Hunter's floor. What she would say to him, she had no idea.

The man obviously despised her. The woman she'd been an hour ago would have been too proud to approach him hat in hand after the way he'd humiliated her. Now pride no longer mattered. Where Bonnie was concerned, she'd discovered that she had no pride.

Disembarking, she hurried to his room, desperately trying to construct a logical argument and failing miserably. The only hope she had was that he hadn't seemed to want Bonnie, while she wanted the baby more than life itself.

But if Trey…Travis wouldn't trust her enough to tell her the truth about what had happened five years ago, how could she dare dream that he would trust her enough to let her raise his daughter?

All she could do was bare her soul to him, tell him why Bonnie was so important to her. Tell him and pray that he'd have enough compassion to at least consider her plea. And if he turned her down…

Andrea's heart refused to consider the possibility.

She approached the room, frowning as she noted Mike Manelli's absence. Why wasn't he here? At any rate, it was lucky for her. It meant there was one less barrier between her and her objective.

Taking a deep breath, Andrea pushed open the door. The air left her lungs in a moan of despair as she found herself staring at a deserted room. The man who called himself Travis Hunter had disappeared again.

Chapter Two

"Am I supposed to believe that Travis checked himself out of the hospital yesterday, then got on board a flight to Europe?"

Mike Manelli leaned his crossed arms on his desk and gave Andrea a smile that had sincerity written all over it. "Would I lie to you?"

"To protect your boss? In a minute."

Manelli gave her a wounded look and swiveled his chair around to appeal to two other employees of Hunter Investigations, Incorporated. "Is Travis in England, or isn't he?"

The gum-chewing, rail-thin Latina looked up from filing her nails. "That's where he called us from this morning."

The middle-aged black man responded with a scowl as big as his paunch. "I took him to the airport myself last night."

Andrea gave them all a look that clearly conveyed

her skepticism. "I suppose he's doing surveillance on Fergie and Di?"

"Actually, he's taking a little vacation. He needs some time off to relax and finish recuperating."

"When is he coming back?"

"He didn't say."

"What number can he be reached at?"

"I'm sorry, but he's not taking any calls. You can leave a message with me, and I'll make sure he gets it."

Andrea stared across the desk at Manelli's handsome, set features and conceded defeat. She was desperate enough to try to buy the information she needed, but she knew that, in this case, it would have been an undeserved insult as well as a waste of time.

Jotting down the number of the portable phone she'd purchased the night before, as well as her home number in Chicago, she placed the scrap of paper on the desk. "Ask your boss to give me a call. It's about his daughter, and it's important."

For the first time, Manelli looked as if she'd said something he hadn't expected to hear. He leaned forward, radar switched on. "The baby? What about her?"

"I'll talk to Travis about that. When he calls."

Giving him a smile that contained more assurance than she felt, Andrea got to her feet, walked out of the office, and shut the door firmly behind her.

Still holding on to her facade of control, she climbed into her rental car and started the engine. Then she closed her eyes and let her head fall forward to rest against the steering wheel. She had nowhere

left to go from here. Nowhere except back to Chicago.
Back to a life that had been stimulating and fulfilling
only days ago, but now seemed empty.

After leaving the hospital in the wake of Travis's
disappearance yesterday, she had purchased the portable phone and every baby-care book she could find.
Then she had returned to her hotel room and read until
she'd fallen into an exhausted sleep.

This morning she'd used the home address listed
under Travis Hunter in the phone book to contact the
manager of his apartment building. But all the man
could tell her was that Mike Manelli had come by with
a key, packed a suitcase full of his boss's clothes and
stopped by the apartment office to tell the manager
that Travis was leaving for England and would be
gone indefinitely.

And now, after she'd finally managed to catch Manelli in his office at the detective agency, she'd only
reached another dead end. All she could do was wait
for Travis to get in touch with her.

On the chance that he would do so, she'd stay in
San Antonio for at least another day.

Having decided on a course of action, she sat up
and put the car into Drive. Then her eyes drifted to
the dashboard clock, and she bore down on the accel-
erator. She did have somewhere to go after all. It was
time to visit Bonnie.

The first thing Andrea noticed as she passed the
nursery window was that Bonnie's crib was empty.
Pushing down a feeling of foreboding, she made her
way back to where the social worker, Janice Murphy,

stood discussing what appeared to be a patient's chart with a nurse.

"Excuse me, I'm here to see Bonnie Hunter."

Ms. Murphy looked up at her with an expression of dismay. "Oh, goodness. Mrs. Emory just left with her. I'm afraid you're too late."

Mrs. Emory? Of course. Travis had signed papers yesterday so that Jenny and Rob Emory would be able to take Bonnie out of the hospital. But Andrea hadn't realized it would happen so soon. Suddenly, she was sure that she had just missed her last chance, that Travis would never contact her, and that Bonnie would be lost to her forever. She could live with having her request for Bonnie turned down, but she had to have the opportunity to plead her case.

The last time she had tried acting it had been an ill-fated venture as the Ghost of Christmas Past in an eighth-grade production of "A Christmas Carol." But she had no choice—instinct told her that she couldn't risk telling the truth. However much she despised dishonesty, she was convinced that it was the only hope she had of finding Bonnie.

"Oh, no!" she exclaimed, struggling to convey emotion after a lifetime spent holding feelings in check. "You mean Jenny left already? But...there must have been a misunderstanding. I was supposed to meet her here and follow her back to her house. Now what am I going to do? I don't even have her address!"

She put a hand up to cover her eyes as if she was on the verge of tears, and found to her surprise that it was nearly true. The stress of the last few days had taken more of a toll than she'd realized.

She breathed a silent prayer of thanks when she felt the social worker's hand on her arm. "There's no need to upset yourself, Ms. Ballanger. The address is right here in Bonnie's chart. I don't know if it's complete, though. It just says Landon Ranch, Layton City, Texas."

Andrea gave her a sincere smile of gratitude. "Thank you. Thank you so much."

She hurried away, thoroughly ashamed of her deception, but not for a second regretting the results it had achieved.

The door of the Landon ranch house swung open and Andrea was confronted by a small, withered gnome of a woman with a skimpy bun of steel gray hair and a scowl that appeared to be set in concrete.

"Is Jenny Emory in?" Andrea asked tentatively.

"No está en casa."

"How about Rob Emory, then?"

"No está en casa."

"When will they be back?"

"No hablo inglés."

Andrea stared at the woman, at a complete loss. Just her luck she had driven all this way only to find a person who made Mike Manelli seem like a font of information.

She tried one more time. "I'm afraid I don't know any Spanish. Do you speak French?" she asked hopefully. *"Parlez-vous franqis?"*

The door shut in her face.

Andrea stared at the weathered wood for a second, then turned away, muttering to herself. "Well, thank you so much for your hospitality. I think I'll just wait out here."

The old porch swing creaked as she sat down, but she sank onto it gratefully. She was tired. Tired from the countless stops she'd had to make in order to ask directions. Tired from driving nearly a hundred miles out to what seemed like the middle of nowhere. She was anxious about Bonnie, and she was sick to death of chasing after phantoms.

Damn Travis Hunter! This was all his fault. Couldn't he have waited just a little longer before he'd disappeared again? How long would it be before he turned up this time? Another five years?

To her surprise that thought…well, it gnawed at her somehow. She told herself it was because she was afraid of losing her only chance to get Bonnie. But, deep down, she knew a part of her fear was that she'd never see Travis again, that she'd never find out the truth of what had happened.

She shifted on the swing, angry that it could still matter to her even a little bit after the way he'd acted in the hospital room. But he hadn't always treated her like that.

Swinging slowly in the sultry summer afternoon, she let her thoughts drift, memories of the past flowing over her like a soft breeze. It had been on a summer day like this in Chicago seven years ago that she'd first met Trey Morgan.

She smiled wryly as she remembered how it had

been. Maybe she should have taken the circumstances of their meeting as an omen of things to come....

Andrea felt a stab of pain as her hip hit the concrete sidewalk. Instinctively, she twisted around and grabbed the long strap of her purse just as it slid free of her shoulder. The would-be robber yanked harder, lifting her half off the sidewalk. Stubbornly, Andrea refused to let go.

"Hold it! Police!"

A larger-than-life man in a blue uniform loomed up behind her attacker. A second later, the purse strap went limp, and the robber was spread-eagled against the outside wall of the exclusive department store Andrea had been about to enter.

Becoming aware of the curious stares of passersby, she struggled to her feet, wincing as she put her weight on her bruised hip. She straightened her clothes and watched as the officer handcuffed the robber, read him his rights and left him in the care of a second officer whose car had just arrived on the scene.

Then her rescuer came toward her, his expression concerned. Andrea felt her heart, which had finally slowed to a near-normal rate, pick up speed again. He was young and strong and handsome. So were many of the eligible men in her own social circle. But he was something they were not. He was real and vital, as alive and as potentially dangerous as the crowded downtown street that bustled around them. And he'd come to her rescue like some knight of old, charging in to save her from harm.

Her own thoughts were enough to make her blush.

After all, the man had only been doing his job. There was nothing even slightly romantic about being a policeman, or about being the victim of a purse snatcher. She was twenty years old, and she was thinking like an adolescent—and even as a child she'd never been given to whimsy. What on earth was wrong with her?

Then he drew closer, and it ceased to matter. She was lost in eyes that were blue seduction.

"Are you all right?" he asked, reaching out to take her arm. She could almost feel his concern increasing as his voice grew softer. "You're shaking. Let's go somewhere where you can sit down and be comfortable."

Wondering if the shaking was a reaction to the attempted robbery or a response to his touch—or maybe a little of both—Andrea let him lead her into the department store. A security guard quickly showed them to a vacant office.

Andrea sank onto one of the plushly upholstered chairs and closed her eyes for a moment, trying to compose herself. When she opened them, the officer was sitting in a chair at her side.

As though it were the most natural thing in the world, he took her hand between both of his larger ones. He held it as if it were made of the finest crystal, as if he were afraid it would shatter at the slightest pressure.

She felt warm skin and what had to be calluses. She'd never known a man with calluses before. She decided that she liked the feel of them.

She managed a smile. "It's all right. I'm not going to faint on you."

His gaze ran over her face, and she felt a sudden rush of physical awareness that she'd never felt before. She had dated quite a few boys in high school and college, but their kisses and passionate propositions had more often amused than aroused her. Now, for the first time in her life, she knew what it was to want a man.

"It's a shame that a lady like you had to go through something like this. Would you like me to take you to the emergency room or your doctor's office?"

"No, I just got the breath knocked out of me. I'm fine now."

"You're sure?"

She nodded reluctantly, and he let go of her hand with what seemed to be an equal amount of regret. "Well, then, if you feel up to it, I need to get some information for my report."

During the next few moments, he found out everything about her: name, address, phone number, birth date. That she had just finished her sophomore year of college as a sociology major at Radcliffe, that she was home for the summer. And that she was unmarried.

She, however, had learned only one thing about him. He didn't like women who went to exclusive colleges and lived in exclusive neighborhoods. His attitude had grown cooler with each question.

Finally, he explained that she would have to stop by the station the next day to give a formal statement and thanked her for her cooperation. Then he stood up to leave.

"And if something like this happens again, Ms. Ballanger, just let the purse go. Fighting back isn't courageous, it's dumb. Especially for someone like you. I'm sure you can easily replace the purse and its contents. Your life isn't replaceable.''

She looked up at him, her anger at his unfair assessment of her and her disappointment at the way things had turned out between them making her uncharacteristically direct.

''Your advice may be perfectly correct, Officer...'' She peered at his name tag. ''Officer Morgan. But your attitude is way out of line. I've seen a lot of snobs in my time, but you have got to be the worst.''

He looked at her as if she'd just said that the earth was flat. ''*Me*, a snob?''

''If a snob is someone who feels superior to another person because of the social class that person belongs to, then, yes, a snob is exactly what you are.''

She got up and limped toward the office door, and he followed, keeping pace with her. ''Maybe I *was* out of line,'' he said grudgingly, sounding as though he hadn't had a lot of practice in admitting he was wrong.

She looked at him in surprise, her resentment fading. ''Apology accepted.''

''Are you going home?'' he asked as she started to open the door.

She paused and looked up at him, risking yet another knee-weakening encounter with those compelling blue eyes. She wanted desperately to go home, to hide in her room until she could come to terms with the newfound awareness of her own vulnerability that the attack had left her with. But to give in to the desire to hide would be to lose a part of the self-control that was so important to her. In her family, no one gave in to their emotions. They suppressed them and carried on.

"No, I'm not going to go home," she heard herself saying. "I'm going to do exactly what I came here to do. Buy a birthday present for my mother and then stop in the restaurant upstairs for a cool drink."

She started to pull the door open again, but he stopped it with his hand. "I go off duty in a couple of hours. I could meet you back here, and we could go out for pizza."

The way he said it was almost a challenge, as if he didn't really think she'd be interested in eating anything that hadn't been sautéed. "It's a date," she told him. "As long as you let me buy the beer."

She went by him quickly, relishing his surprised expression, but afraid he would somehow discover that she'd never had a beer in her life.

Her parents would certainly disapprove of the dashing Officer Morgan, but she had spent her entire life doing things that her parents approved of. It was high time she did something that she *wanted* to do. Besides, it was only one date.

Three weeks later, they were married. Andrea, who hadn't been sure she believed in love before she'd met Trey, had fallen so deeply in love that nothing else mattered.

Stunned by her defiance, her parents refused to speak to her. They sent the butler to the phone to tell her she would only be welcome in their home again when she came to her senses and divorced that "pen-

niless fortune hunter'' she'd had the poor taste to
marry.

Trey had expected more understanding from his uncle, Fred Henderson, who had raised him from the
time Trey was fifteen. A Chicago policeman, Fred had
been proud to have his sister's son follow in his footsteps. But he hadn't been proud of Trey's marriage to
Andrea. ''It will never work,'' he'd told Trey. ''She's
way outta your league.''

But for once, Andrea didn't care what anyone else
thought. She had Trey, and he had her.

As a child she had lain awake at night longing for
warm, loving parents instead of the cool, emotionally
distant pair that fate had given her. She vowed it
would be different for her own children. She and Trey
would show them what love was. Together they would
create the close, caring family that she had always
wanted.

Her wedding night was all she had ever dreamed it
would be. Trey was an experienced, giving lover. The
chemistry between them was explosive. Andrea became a being of pure feeling, unable to hold anything
back. She was shocked at the height of passion she
was capable of reaching. There was no part of her that
she could deny Trey, no part of him that she didn't
long to possess. She had never been so happy.

After the honeymoon, Trey moved out of his uncle's apartment, and they rented a small place in a
borderline neighborhood. They could have afforded
better, but the lower rent allowed Andrea to continue
her college education at a Chicago university and

made it possible for them to put something aside each month for the house they someday hoped to own.

Andrea tried hard not to resent the fact that Trey stubbornly refused to let her use the money from her grandfather's trust fund to help pay the bills. She tried to learn how to budget, to live on a policeman's salary.

When she used money that should have gone toward the light bill to splurge on lobster and champagne for their first month's anniversary, the lights were turned off. They had their first real argument: Trey shouted at her, and Andrea retreated to her room to hide her tears.

He came to her later, and they made wild, passionate love in the dark. Without ever discussing it, they somehow reached a compromise. She used her own money to pay the bill, and Trey let it pass without comment or protest.

But despite their continuing physical closeness, Andrea began to feel the same familiar loneliness that had plagued her all her life. Like her parents, Trey never confided his deepest feelings, never talked about how the terrible things he must be seeing each day affected him. And she discovered that though she had resented her parents' aloofness, she had learned to behave just like them. She was a prisoner of self-imposed restraints, not knowing quite how to tell Trey how alone she felt and how much she worried about the dangers he faced on the job.

After he brushed aside her first few tentative attempts at real communication, she stopped trying. Trey still responded to her in bed, still made her feel loved and cherished. She began to believe that she was expecting too much of marriage. As a sociology major, she knew that an ideal oneness of shared thoughts and feelings was a romantic concept that just didn't exist in the real world.

Maybe her feeling that something was lacking just meant that it was time to have a baby. She only had a few months left until she received her degree and, when they had discussed children, Trey had left the timing up to her. A baby would make them a real family. It would give her and Trey experiences to share that would bring them closer together. And it would fill the emptiness inside her that no amount of lovemaking—or studying—seemed to banish.

For a while, she was happy with her decision, sure that now that she had more realistic expectations everything was going to work out between her and Trey, after all. And it did. Until the night that he came home, his eyes red rimmed and filled with despair.

"Uncle Fred was shot on the job today. He saw something go down that he shouldn't have seen, and now he's dead."

Andrea gave a wordless exclamation of dismay and rushed forward to put her arms around her husband. She had liked Trey's uncle. Despite his prejudice against her, he had never turned his back on them as her own parents had. Now, in the blink of an eye, Fred Henderson was gone. His death reinforced all her unspoken fears about the dangers inherent in a policeman's job.

She held Trey tightly, longing for him to reassure her, longing for him to share his grief with her so that she could ease it. Surely, he would need her now. But his body was stiff and unyielding in her arms. She could feel his tightly leashed anger.

"The man who killed my uncle is going to pay for what he did. I went right to the top for approval. After the funeral, I'm going undercover."

Andrea looked up at him, worried eyes searching his, silently pleading with him to say more. But instead, his mouth came down to cover hers with a passion that was close to frenzied.

He scooped her up in his arms and carried her into the bedroom. Once there, his lovemaking was wild and desperate, and over as quickly as it had begun.

Andrea lay in their bed, physically sated, but emotionally starved, and watched as her husband disengaged himself from her arms. He got up and went into the living room to grieve alone while, once again, she cried her silent tears.

For their marriage, it had been the beginning of the end.

"Can I help you, ma'am?"

Andrea pulled herself back from the past, surprised by the fresh pain that lingered in the wake of her old memories. That was another thing she could blame Travis for. Seeing him had made it all real to her again.

She looked at the young cowboy who was standing in the ranch yard and smiling at her from across the porch railing that separated them. Despite her gloomy thoughts, she couldn't help but return his smile. His could have melted a polar ice cap—and he wasn't half trying.

She got up off of the swing, smoothing her skirt into place. "I must be slipping. I didn't even hear a car."

"I left my horse over by the barn." He came up the porch steps to stand in front of her. "I'm Rob Emory," he said, offering her his hand.

"I'm Andrea Ballanger from Chicago," she said, silently thankful that, despite his muscular build, his grip was gentle. She took a deep breath and told him the story that had worked for her at the hospital. "I'm a relative of Travis Hunter's."

"I didn't know old Trav had any family willing to claim him," he said, moving past her toward the door. "Well, come on inside and have a cold drink. What are you doing sitting out here in the heat?"

"The…the older lady who answered the door…that is, she…"

His chuckle interrupted her before she could decide how best to describe her reception. "Lupe isn't exactly what you'd call a ray of sunshine, is she? Her daughter's our regular cook, but she broke her arm. Lupe's substituting for her. No one's real happy with the arrangement—least of all Lupe."

The sound of an approaching car engine made them both turn and look toward the road. A covered Jeep moved up the long driveway and came to a stop a few feet from the porch. A slender, redheaded woman wearing jeans and a blouse climbed out.

Even from the vantage point of the porch, it was obvious to Andrea that the other woman had not had an easy day. Her drawn expression and the way she rubbed at her neck conveyed her tiredness as clearly as any words could have.

Andrea followed Rob down the steps, her heart beating faster in anticipation as she saw the baby carrier in the passenger seat of the Jeep.

"This is my wife, Jenny," Rob said, making the necessary introductions. "Jenny, this is Andrea Ballanger, one of Travis's family from Chicago."

Thankfully, Jenny appeared too weary to ask for any details. She nodded vaguely in Andrea's direction and reached for the baby carrier.

"Could I take her?" Andrea asked.

The other woman studied Andrea's face for a moment, then shrugged. "Sure, why not?"

Andrea released the seat belt and picked up the carrier. She looked down, drinking in the sight of the sleeping baby. She felt some of the anxiety leave her now that she was actually with Bonnie again. But she knew nothing had really been accomplished yet. If she didn't get in touch with Travis, this could be the last time she'd ever see the baby.

Jenny leaned over the carrier, straightening the blanket around Bonnie's face. "She's a good baby," she said with a soft voice that held obvious affection. "She slept all morning—thank God."

Rob looked down at the precious bundle Andrea held and gently stroked a lock of the baby's hair. "She sure is a pretty little thing. Just like her mama was."

The couple exchanged a look that held enough poignancy to bring a lump to Andrea's throat. Then the moment passed.

Rob took the diaper bag and other baby supplies as

Jenny reached past Andrea into the Jeep and retrieved what looked like a doctor's black bag. Then Andrea saw Jennifer Landon Emory, D.V.M., stamped on the bag in gold letters and realized that Jenny was a veterinarian.

"Have you been working today, Jenny?" she asked, wondering where the woman had found the time.

Jenny nodded and updated them on the morning's events as they all moved toward the house. "I'd barely gotten back from the hospital and gotten the baby fed, when the girl who was supposed to baby-sit for us called. She said she got a job in a bank in San Antonio and wouldn't be coming after all. As soon as I hung up, Dwight Newsome called. That mare his daughter uses for barrel racing somehow got caught up in a fence and gashed her side. Naturally, Lupe refused to take care of the baby while I went out—said we hired her as a cook, not a…"

She looked at her husband, apparently waiting for him to supply the Spanish word.

"Baby-sitter?" Rob suggested, his eyes twinkling mischievously.

Jenny gave a long-suffering sigh, but she smiled for the first time since she'd gotten out of the car. Her smile soon turned into a worried frown again. "Luckily, Dwight's daughter agreed to keep an eye on Bonnie while I sewed up the mare. But I don't know what I'm going to do for a baby-sitter from now on."

Rob looked thoughtful. "What about Maggie?" he asked, adding for Andrea's benefit, "Maggie is my brother Jude's wife."

Jenny shook her head. "Maggie has a new baby of

her own and an older child to worry about—not to mention ten dude-ranch guests to entertain.''

"Too bad Mama's not here," Rob said. "She'd be glad to help out." He looked at Andrea as he held open the front door for her. "My mother came into some money recently and decided to travel and see the world.''

"Good for her," Andrea told him as she moved past him into the house. Her head was whirling with the effort of keeping up with all the conversation about relatives, but the idea of having a large, close-knit family seemed wonderful to her.

The cool, air-conditioned ranch house felt like heaven as she followed Jenny down the hall. The home was clean, but definitely lived in, with a rustic charm that Andrea found very appealing. Somehow she felt...*welcomed,* that was the word.

"This used to be my mama and daddy's room," Jenny said as they entered what could only be called a nursery. "Mama died when I was little, and Daddy passed away last year.''

"I'm sorry to hear that," Andrea murmured automatically as she studied the room. It had been painted a bright shade of yellow and had a Sesame Street mural covering one wall. The crib, mobile, changing table and other baby items reflected the same theme. It all looked so planned, so *permanent,* that her heart sank.

"You must have had to work hard to get all this ready in time for Bonnie's discharge," she commented.

"Actually, I didn't find out I'd be taking care of Bonnie until a few days ago when Travis called me from the hospital and asked me if I'd do it. Rob and I had already put together this room for the baby I'm going to have about six months from now.''

Andrea felt her hopes skyrocket again. ''Congratulations,'' she said, sincerely happy for Jenny—and relieved that she might still be in the running as far as Bonnie was concerned. She set the baby carrier inside the crib and started to undo the strap.

Jenny's whisper stopped her. ''Don't disturb her. She's comfortable enough in there. I'll take her out as soon as she wakes up. Come on.''

The other woman led the way out of the room, and Andrea followed reluctantly. She would have liked nothing better than to sit and watch Bonnie as she slept, but she reminded herself that there were other priorities. Such as locating Travis Hunter.

When they entered the dining room, they found Rob placing glasses of ice tea and a plate of sandwiches on the long rectangular table while conversing with Lupe in what sounded to Andrea like fluent Spanish.

''I wish I had your facility with languages,'' she told him as Lupe returned to the kitchen and they all seated themselves around the table.

''Can't claim any credit for that,'' Rob said. ''My mama was born in Mexico.''

For the first time, Andrea noticed his golden skin and dark eyes. ''So that's where you get all that charm,'' she said teasingly.

Jenny gave her a look over the top of her glass. ''Please, don't encourage him. His ego is getting too big to fit in the house as it is.''

Rob just grinned. "Don't you listen to her, Andrea. You can compliment me all you want."

Jenny heaved an exasperated sigh before she gave in and smiled, too. "What are you doing home, anyway?" she asked her husband. "Aren't you supposed to be out with our guests?"

"I snuck away for a few minutes to see how you were doing and if Bonnie got here okay."

"Rob," Jenny said reproachfully, "those city people are liable to kill themselves alone out there."

"It's the cattle I feel sorry for," Rob retorted. He responded to Andrea's puzzled look. "We have five dude-ranch guests for the week."

"My husband's brother, Jude, and Jude's wife, Maggie, own another ranch near here," Jenny chimed in. "Most of the guests stay with them at the Double Diamond ranch house. It's a mansion compared to this. There's a swimming pool, and a TV in every room. Here, we take the dudes who want to rough it. They stay in the old bunkhouse we remodeled, and they participate in more actual ranch work than the guests at the Double Diamond."

Rob shook his head. "I'll never understand why people would want to pay to spend their vacation working."

He popped the remainder of his sandwich into his mouth and stood up just as the cook came out of the kitchen. She passed by them, muttered a few words in Spanish and disappeared down the hallway.

"Lupe's gone to lie down and take her siesta," Rob explained in response to Jenny's inquiring look.

"When you're her age, you'll probably need one, too."

Jenny put her empty glass down on the table. "I need one now."

Rob gave her a concerned look as he picked up his Stetson. "I'll be glad to take care of Bonnie if you want to get out of the house and ride herd on our guests."

"Thanks, but no thanks. All in all, I think Bonnie's the easier job. And at least the house is air-conditioned."

"I tried." He bent down to give Jenny a kiss that heated the room several degrees. "I'll see you later."

"Is that a promise?"

"Oh, yeah."

"Good. I'll hold you to it."

Andrea felt a pang of envy at the couple's obvious happiness. But she returned Rob's smile as he turned toward her.

"Andrea, I hope to see you again before you go back to Illinois. If not, it was nice meeting you."

The front door closed behind him and there was a heartbeat of silence—followed by the sound of a baby wailing.

Jenny pushed to her feet with an obvious effort.

"What can I do to help?" Andrea asked.

"Why don't you go change her and bring her out while I get a bottle ready."

Andrea almost flew to the nursery and smiled down into the unhappy little face that greeted her. "Let's get you out of that carrier, precious."

She found a disposable diaper and went through the

motions of changing the baby, frustrated by her own awkwardness. She had no practical experience with children. But the nurses had showed her how to feed and burp Bonnie yesterday in the hospital nursery, and she had taken a baby-care course years ago. She pushed away the inevitable sadness that thought brought with it.

Baby-care theory she had down pat. All she needed now was the experience. She could only hope that she'd have the opportunity to acquire it.

Carefully, she picked Bonnie up and, holding her securely in her arms, carried her out to the living room. She sat down in the rocking chair there just as Jenny came out of the kitchen with a bottle of formula.

"Is it okay if I feed her?" Andrea asked hopefully.

Jenny handed her the bottle and sat down on the nearby sofa. She watched in silence for a moment before asking a question that caused Andrea's heart to skip a beat. "Just how are you related to Travis Hunter?"

Andrea looked up at the other woman, feeling like an animal caught in a trap. She didn't want to lie, but she had no idea how much Travis had told Jenny about his past. And she didn't want to do anything to jeopardize her chances with Bonnie.

Finally, she decided all she could do was follow her instincts and tell the truth. "Actually, I'm Travis's ex-wife."

Jenny's eyes widened as if that were the last answer she'd expected. "Travis never mentioned he'd been married before Lissa."

"I'm sure he'd like to forget he ever was," Andrea said with a hint of bitterness.

"It doesn't sound like you've stayed friends."

"Until yesterday, I hadn't seen him since the divorce five years ago. I was in Chicago—I teach sociology at a university there—when I came across an old newspaper clipping about the shooting in the mall. There were a lot of things left unresolved between Travis and me at the time of our divorce, and I felt..."

She shifted Bonnie in her arms, trying to find words to describe her feelings and failing. "I felt I had to come to see him. But, when I showed up at the hospital, we argued and I left the room to cool off. The hospital social worker was elated to find what she thought was an interested family member. She practically dragged me off to see Bonnie. I wasn't expecting to feel anything, but I fell in love with her at first sight."

"You argued with Travis?" Jenny asked, her expression thoughtful. "He actually came out of that trance he's been in for a month?"

"Trance?" Andrea echoed.

"He hasn't really responded to anything since the shooting. He refused to even see the baby." Jenny leaned toward Andrea, her gaze direct. "I don't want you to misunderstand what I'm about to say. I truly don't mind taking care of Lissa's little girl while Travis is recuperating—and longer if need be. Lissa and I were friends since we were toddlers, and I loved her dearly. It's just that I've been getting the feeling that Travis considers this a permanent arrangement. What happened in that mall was a terrible tragedy—a tragedy that affected all of us. But if I took Bonnie, I feel like I'd be enabling Travis to keep on grieving forever. I'd be helping him to turn his back on his own baby without even trying to be a daddy to her. And that's just not right for him or for her. Lissa wouldn't have wanted that.''

Andrea ignored the voice inside her that said Jenny was right. Jenny had just confirmed what she had been feeling all along. Travis didn't want to raise Bonnie. She told herself that that was the only thing that mattered.

''I know that you're probably right,'' Andrea said, pressing onward. ''But I also know that once Travis makes up his mind to do something, it would take a convoy of bulldozers to change it. To be honest with you, Bonnie is the whole reason I'm here. When I talked to Travis in the hospital, I came to the same conclusion you did. Whatever his motive, he isn't planning to raise this baby. I can't...I don't have any children, and, when I saw Bonnie in the hospital, I knew I wanted her. I'd like very much to adopt her.''

Having finally said the words aloud, Andrea felt a sense of relief. But at Jenny's next question, her apprehension returned full force.

''Have you already talked to Travis about this?''

Andrea heard a noise and looked down at Bonnie. To her surprise, the bottle was empty. She set it aside and raised the baby to her shoulder, patting her back gently. ''When I returned to his hospital room after seeing Bonnie yesterday, I was told he'd signed himself out against doctor's orders. I didn't know where he'd gone so I came to you, the lady Bonnie was released to, hoping you could tell me where he is.''

Jenny regarded her in silence, her gaze traveling from Andrea's face to the baby she held in her arms. Finally, she appeared to come to a decision.

''By now, Travis should be near here, in Layton City. He called me last night and said he was coming over from San Antonio. He said he'd already signed himself out of the hospital, and that he intended to spend the next couple of weeks recuperating in peace and quiet in the old house Lissa's parents left to her. She and Travis put it up for sale after they got married and moved to San Antonio, but there haven't been any buyers yet.''

''Can you tell me how to get there?'' Andrea asked.

''I'll do better than that. I'll take you there. I have a few things to say to Travis Hunter myself. If that man is going to give up this baby, he's damned well going to see her first.''

Given the circumstances, Andrea would have much preferred talking to Travis in private, but she could think of no graceful way to exclude Jenny. The other woman had already retrieved the baby seat. Resigned to the situation, Andrea placed the baby in the carrier.

Hopefully, Travis would behave more civilly than he had in the hospital. After Jenny had had her say, she would ask to talk to him alone, to explain why she needed Bonnie. If he had any good memories of the past, he would understand. He would agree to her request. She didn't want to think about what would happen if she was wrong.

* * *

The first thing that Andrea noticed as they pulled up to the house was that there was no car outside.

"It looks deserted, doesn't it?" Jenny said, worry in her voice. "Travis should have gotten here way before now."

"Maybe he just went out for groceries or something," Andrea suggested. "Maybe his car's inside the garage."

"Or maybe something went wrong."

Both women twisted around to look at Bonnie. The baby was sleeping peacefully in her carrier.

Andrea saw her chance to have a moment alone with Travis—if indeed he was in the house. She touched Jenny's arm. "Don't disturb Bonnie for no reason. Let me check first and see if Travis is even there."

"Good idea." Jenny pulled her keys out of the ignition, isolated a particular key and held it out to Andrea. "If no one answers the door, go in and see if there's any sign that he's arrived. If he hasn't, I'm calling the sheriff. Travis shouldn't have left the hospital early. Anything could have happened to him on the road."

Beginning to feel a little worried herself, Andrea got out of the car and started up what once must have been a flower-bordered walk. The blossoms had wilted to dry stalks due to the heat and an obvious lack of care.

She pushed the doorbell, but heard no chimes. Raising her hand, she knocked forcefully once, twice. After a moment, when there was no response, she took the key that Jenny had given her and inserted it into the lock.

The door swung open, and Andrea walked inside, closing it behind her. It was so hot in the house that it felt like an oven. Travis couldn't be in here. No one could live in this heat!

She flipped a wall switch and confirmed the suspicion that had formed in her mind when the doorbell had failed to sound. There was no electricity.

Now she held out little hope that she'd find evidence that anyone had been staying here, but she wanted to be able to report to Jenny that she'd made a thorough search.

Her clothes were beginning to stick to her skin when she entered the hallway and pushed open the first door. It revealed a bedroom that contained a bedroom set with no sheets or any other indication that the house was anything but vacant.

The second door opened into a small bathroom that was just as barren. She hurried to the last door, anxious to complete the useless task and get out of the stifling heat.

She put her hand on the doorknob, pushed the door open and found herself staring down the barrel of a gun.

"Oh!" She came to an abrupt halt, one hand going to her throat in alarm. Her heart seemed to ricochet off her rib cage, and her knees felt as if they were going to buckle. Then her eyes focused on the man behind the gun. When she saw that it was Travis Hunter, her terror turned to anger.

"This," she said disdainfully, "is the best argument for gun control that I have ever seen."

He stood there clad only in a pair of black jockey

shorts and a bandage, sweat beading his chest and forehead. Swaying on his feet, he lowered the gun. "If I was smart," he said in a voice laden with disgust, "I'd shoot you while I had the chance."

She watched as the gun slipped slowly from his fingers and dropped onto the rug at her feet. Then, before she could move to prevent it, he crumpled forward and followed it down.

Chapter Three

Travis felt a cool, soft hand slip beneath his neck. His head was lifted up slightly, and something hard pressed against his mouth. He opened his lips under the pressure, and a cold, sweet liquid flowed over his tongue. He swallowed greedily.

Floating in a timeless haze, he opened his eyes and focused on the face so close to his. *Andrea*. His Andrea. So remote and untouchable. Until you touched her, and she turned to fire in your arms. He'd missed touching her.

He raised one hand and let it trace the shape of her cheek. "You aren't really here, are you?"

Her forehead creased in what looked like concern. "Of course I am."

Suddenly, he awakened fully, his sense of time dropping firmly into place. Andrea wasn't his wife anymore; she was his ex-wife. One very persistent and annoying ex-wife.

Feeling like a fool, he tried to cover his earlier reaction. "You're real? Damn. I was hoping it was a bad dream."

Despite his resolve to remain unmoved by the woman in front of him, he almost smiled at the look that came over her face. It was as if she had bitten into something sour and was too polite to spit it out.

His amusement faded as the circumstances of their last meeting came back to him. He took a quick visual survey of the room and realized that it was evening, and that he was no longer at the house in town. He was at Landon Ranch, Rob and Jenny's place.

"How did I get here?" he asked, struggling to sit up.

He felt a surge of alarm when the gentle pressure of Andrea's hand against his chest was all that was needed to hold him in place.

Andrea left her hand pressed against his warm skin for an instant longer than necessary until she remembered herself and hastily removed it. Whatever else might have died between them, the sexual attraction she used to feel was alive and well. For someone who prided herself on control, the situation was unnerving.

Clearing her throat, she tried to answer his question. "When you passed out at the house in town, I wrapped a sheet around you and managed to get you up and help you to Jenny's car. We left your car in the garage. Jenny said it would be safe there."

Fuzzy memories played around the edges of his consciousness, but he had no clear recollection of the incident. He did have the feeling that he was missing some vital facts. How had Andrea and Jenny gotten together? And why had Jenny felt it necessary to bring him all the way out here to her ranch? But, at the moment, he had a more important question on his mind. "Just how did you find out that I was staying in Layton City?"

"While I was in your hospital room, I overheard that Jenny and Rob Emory were going to take Bonnie. The social worker gave me their address. When I got here, Jenny told me where to find you."

Travis cursed under his breath. If Andrea could find him that way, then someone else could follow the same trail. This woman could have led his enemies straight to him. Straight to all of them!

His voice came out low and hard. "Just why in hell did you follow—?"

The sound of a shrill whistle cut him off in mid-sentence. He started, his hands automatically reaching for his gun. But his gun and shoulder holster had disappeared. All he was wearing was a pajama bottom.

"It's just the teakettle," Andrea told him. Glad of the reprieve—from both his hostility and her all too predictable reaction to him—she forced herself to her feet. "Would you like a cup?"

Travis looked up at her, his expression foretelling a negative response. "All I want from you is my gun and an explanation of what you're doing here!"

The whistling sound increased in intensity, and Andrea fled toward the door. "I've got to get that before it wakes the baby."

"Let someone else get it!" he yelled after her as she disappeared through the bedroom doorway.

She stuck her head back in. "Jenny and Rob are

both over at the Double Diamond, and Lupe—the cook—has gone to visit her sick daughter. There is no one else.''

Before he could respond, she had vanished again.

Travis lay in the big bed, his body at rest, his mind working double-time. What was Andrea doing here? What had she told Rob and Jenny? And what was she doing taking care of the baby? None of it made any sense to him.

Vowing to pry the answers to those questions out of Andrea as soon as she returned, he put the mystery aside momentarily and reached for the bedside phone. He dialed his phone credit card number from memory along with the number for Hunter Investigations.

''Mike Manelli. How can I help you?''

''Mike, it's Travis. Remember Janice Murphy, that social worker at the hospital? Apparently, she gave Jenny and Rob Emory's address to Andrea Ballanger.''

Mike gave a soft whistle of admiration that somehow grated on Travis's nerves. ''That is one determined lady. She was here earlier today trying to find out where you were. You want the number to her portable phone?''

''No,'' Travis said dryly, ''I think I know where to get in touch with her. What I want you to do is check with that social worker and see if she gave the address to anyone else—or if anyone else has asked about it.''

''I don't know if she'll be working this late. You want to hold while I call the hospital on the other line?''

Travis listened to elevator music for five minutes

before Mike got back to him. "Everything's okay. The social worker said she told no one but Andrea Ballanger where your daughter was taken, and no one else has asked. She said she'd write on the chart that the information is strictly confidential and not to be given out to anyone. Want me to call Gonzalez at the police station and see if they can have the hospital delete the information entirely?"

"Sounds good to me," Travis told him, feeling a lot more secure than he had a moment before. "After you're through with that, I have some investigative work for you to do."

"Out of town?"

"Uh-huh. I want you to spend a couple of weeks in Chicago...."

Travis hung up the phone just seconds before Andrea came back into the room carrying a tray of soup and sandwiches.

"I made a snack for you," she said, avoiding his gaze. "You must be hungry by now."

As she bent over to place the tray on the bedside table, Travis found himself staring at the shadowy hint of cleavage revealed by the neckline of her silk blouse. Staring and remembering just how soft her breasts felt and how they responded to his fingers...his mouth....

He felt his body growing hard and turned his head away as abruptly as if she had slapped him—which she would probably have done if she could have read his thoughts. So he still wanted her. Why shouldn't he? The sexual side of their marriage had been better than great. But the marriage itself had ended up almost destroying him.

Angry at his own unpredictable responses, he channeled that anger at its cause. "I don't know what this is all about, Andrea. But you're going to tell me. *Now.*"

Andrea felt his anger and it stoked her own. "All right, I'll tell you. But first I want to hear you say that you're Trey Morgan."

Travis glared at her with five years' worth of resentment and hostility. "Okay, I admit it. I was once Trey Morgan. But that part of my life is over. That man is dead. The subject is closed."

"No, it's not," Andrea insisted, struggling to assert herself. "You owe me an explanation."

"I don't owe you a damned thing!" he yelled, letting out all the pain and frustration that he'd been hoarding. "My obligations to you ended the day you filed for divorce."

The truth of those words hit Andrea like a physical blow. "I had my reasons," she said.

"Well, Travis Hunter doesn't want to hear them, and Trey Morgan is dead."

Hurt welled up in Andrea. After all this time, he was still refusing to listen to her. Her thoughts spilled out into words. "Somehow, some way, you could have had the common decency to let me know that you were still alive."

"And you could have had the decency to wait and tell me face-to-face that you wanted a divorce. Or, at the very least, to leave a note behind to explain for you. If you had something to say to me, you should have said it then. It's too late now.''

He was right. But then, the last time she'd left their apartment, it was in an ambulance on its way to the hospital. She hadn't had time to write a note or even think about one. And later on, she'd been filled with too much anger and bitterness to care. And now? Now, telling him wouldn't change what had happened, or save a marriage that had ended years ago. Obviously, the most positive thing this man would have left to give her was his pity, and she didn't want or need that. She suddenly realized that she wouldn't be able to bear it.

''This is a waste of time and breath,'' she said, believing it. ''It was all over between us a long time ago.''

''For once we're in complete agreement.'' He'd been hurt enough by this woman. He wasn't ever going to let her put him in that position again. ''But if you feel that way, then why in hell did you follow me here?''

Andrea felt her temper flare. It was clear he couldn't stand the sight of her. She had to fight to keep her voice level. ''I'm here because I saw your daughter in the hospital. I didn't plan to—it was the social worker's idea. But once I saw Bonnie, well, I fell in love with her. I've decided I'd like to adopt her.''

Travis would have been less surprised if she'd leapt up on top of the dresser and started to tap-dance. Somehow, in some small corner of his heart he didn't even want to acknowledge, he had cherished the idea of Andrea's seeking him out and following him because she still had feelings for him. It had been like an unexpected but tempting gift that he couldn't afford to keep and didn't dare open. Now she was saying it was his daughter she wanted? He felt like a fool. A very angry fool.

"Adopt my daughter? Not on your best day, lady! You're just a spoiled, rich debutante who wants a new toy to play with. And when you're sick of playing mommy, you'll stick her in some boarding school and forget about her...." *Just like you forgot about me!* he almost added. But he caught himself in time. "Go back to Chicago and have a child of your own!"

Andrea kept her face expressionless, determined not to reveal the pain his words had caused. Did he really think so little of her? She was about to speak again, to try once more to reason with him, when the sound of the front door opening distracted her.

She couldn't decide whether she welcomed the interruption or not. She wanted to continue pleading her case, but she seemed to be losing more ground with every word she spoke. Maybe it would be better if they both took the time to cool down first.

Avoiding Travis's gaze, she waited for the others to come to them. And she tried not to give in to despair. She hadn't lost Bonnie yet.

Seconds later, Jenny and Rob led the way into the room. A little boy and two adults—one carrying a baby in her arms—followed after them.

Jenny introduced the visitors to Andrea. "This is my brother-in-law Jude Emory, his wife Maggie, and their son Todd. And this," she said, cooing to the blanket-wrapped bundle in the other woman's arms, "is their daughter, Karyn."

Her attention drawn like steel to a magnet, Andrea leaned over the baby. "How old is she?" she asked, automatically looking to the mother for the answer.

She felt her mouth drop open slightly in amazement. Even dressed in jeans and an old shirt, without any visible traces of makeup, Maggie Emory was the most beautiful woman Andrea had ever seen. A face framed with blond curls, huge green eyes and peaches-and-cream skin that didn't have one visible pore.

Maggie gave her a dimpled smile that revealed perfect teeth and a warm acceptance of Andrea's reaction to her appearance. "Karyn will be three months old next week."

Her husband gave a long-suffering sigh. "And it's been a long three months. I haven't had a decent night's sleep since she was born."

For the first time, Andrea really looked at the man that Maggie had married. She was surprised to see that Jude Emory was as homely as his wife was beautiful. There was a ridge of scar tissue bisecting one side of his face, but he had his brother Rob's handsome, expressive eyes.

Andrea gave him a smile before lowering her gaze to the little boy standing so close to his father's side. "And how old are you?"

Todd looked up at her guilelessly, his face the image of his mother's. "I'm eight," he said proudly. "And I'll be in third grade next year."

"Good for you," Andrea told him.

She watched as the boy left his father and ran over

to the bed. "Hi, Uncle Travis! Did you really get shot in the chest?"

Maggie groaned aloud. *"Todd Emory!"*

Jenny gave the other woman a quick glance of empathy. But Travis only smiled. The sight of that smile—knowing that he would never smile for her like that again—tore at her heart.

Travis pulled down the bedcovers to reveal the large square of bandage. "I sure did."

"Wow!" Todd exclaimed, clearly impressed by his "uncle's" powers of endurance. Then his expression sobered. "Aunt Lissa got shot, too, but she died."

Maggie took a step forward, but she halted when Jude put a hand on her shoulder.

Travis's smile faded, and he looked up at Todd's small, earnest face. "Yes, she did die."

"I liked her," the boy told him. "She was nice, and she made me laugh."

"Me, too," Travis said, reaching up to tousle Todd's blond curls.

Apparently satisfied with the exchange, Todd turned back to his mother. "Can I go watch TV now?"

Obviously relieved, Maggie nodded. "Go ahead. You know where it is."

As the boy disappeared from the room, Maggie sank onto a chair, still holding her sleeping daughter. "I swear that boy is going to give me a heart attack someday! I'm sorry about that, Travis. Are you okay?"

"I'm fine," Travis told her, believing it.

Both of Jenny's hands went to her hips. "Fine for someone we had to scrape up off the floor, you mean. You are very lucky that I didn't take you right back to that hospital. What on earth were you thinking of to sign yourself out in your condition?''

That if an amateur like Andrea Ballanger could find me, I needed a safer place to stay, Travis thought, shooting his ex-wife an irritated glance. But that wasn't the answer he gave Jenny. ''I was sick of being confined in that hospital with everyone poking and prodding me.''

Jenny gave him a narrow look. ''Is that right?''

''I just got a little dizzy this morning, that's all. You didn't need to kidnap me. I could have stayed in that house and taken care of myself.''

He moved to get up, to prove that his words were true. He was amazed at the feeling of weakness that rushed over him. The room tilted, and he put his head back down on the pillow with a groan of defeat.

The three women exchanged looks that contained equal amounts of amusement and exasperation.

''Kidnapped?'' Jenny echoed. ''Rescued is more like it. What were you doing running around playing cops and robbers in that sweltering house?''

''The lights were scheduled to be turned on tomorrow. And I wasn't playing cops and robbers. The sound Andrea made coming into the house woke me from a dead sleep. I wasn't even sure where I was.''

''Well, you're here now. Dr. Hooper stopped by earlier and examined you. He said you had a fever and were probably dehydrated. He gave you a shot and prescribed plenty of fluids and at least two weeks of rest. He also said that if you didn't follow his orders, he was going to give you another shot—one that would knock you out until 'hell froze over.' ''

"That's a bluff if I ever heard one," Travis blustered, privately sure that the bossy old quack was quite capable of using such methods—and of enjoying every minute of it.

"If you're not smart enough to comply with those orders of your own free will," Jenny told him, "then Rob and Jude have been deputized to enforce them."

Travis looked at his two friends as though expecting them to deny it, but they only nodded.

"Traitors," he muttered.

The two brothers looked at each other, then back at him. "That about covers it," Rob agreed. "We know when to fight and when to go along. And this is definitely go-along time. Doc Hooper is bad enough, but our wives..."

Rob gave an exaggerated shudder that earned him an elbow in the ribs from Jenny.

He turned toward Travis with a grin. "Aw, come on, don't lie there pretending you have it so tough. If I had a pretty lady like Andrea bringing me dinner trays, I'd be dreaming up ways to stay sick for as long as I could."

Travis looked at Andrea, a little surprised to find she was still there. She had blended in so well, her presence had seemed perfectly natural. And that worried him more than any "hot flashes" she'd been giving him. It was time that she went back to her own world, where she belonged—before he got too used to having her around.

If there was anything he'd learned about Andrea during two years of marriage, it was that she had a horror of drawing attention to herself. So far, she'd surprised him by refusing to back down from fighting with him in private, but he was sure she would leave rather than cause a scene in front of virtual strangers.

"Andrea won't be here to bring me any more trays," he said coolly. "In fact, she was just leaving."

The warm atmosphere of friendship and caring that had filled the room dissipated abruptly. Andrea felt its absence keenly. She had finally caught a glimpse of something she had been looking for all her life only to have it disappear before she had a chance to savor it. The anger and apprehension she felt toward Travis turned into defiance.

She met his gaze levelly. "Before I go, I'd like another few minutes alone with you to talk about Bonnie."

There was something in her eyes that was so compelling that he almost agreed to her request, but then he remembered the past and hardened his heart. "I already gave you my answer. I won't change my mind."

Andrea hesitated, every instinct protesting against revealing such a private part of herself in front of a roomful of people, no matter how sympathetic they might be. But if a public hearing was her only alternative, then she would take it.

Ignoring her misgivings, she continued speaking. "I've formed an attachment to Bonnie. I care about her. I didn't expect it, and I didn't ask for it to happen. But since you don't seem to want her—"

Travis struggled to a sitting position, his face set, obviously furious. "Like I said before, that's none of your business."

"I *do* want her. I think that makes it my business."

"What is this, some twisted form of revenge for the way things turned out between us?"

"Not at all. I'm very serious. I want Bonnie."

"No way in hell."

Andrea stood there in the ensuing silence, having reached a dead end once more. What could she do to change his mind? All that she could think of was the words he'd hurled at her earlier: *You're just a spoiled, rich debutante who wants a new toy to play with. And when you're sick of playing mommy, you'll stick her in some boarding school and forget about her....*

She saw only one way to change that opinion. "What if I can prove to you that I'm worthy of Bonnie, that I truly want her? Prove it by caring for you and the baby without complaint until you're well again. If you still feel the same way then, I'll abide by your decision. You will have lost nothing, and Jenny will have gained the services of a free baby-sitter for the interim. The only one who stands to lose anything if you accept is me."

Travis couldn't have thought of a plan better designed to torment him. If he was wavering now, after only a few hours of contact with her, how much resistance would he have left after two weeks of being exposed to her presence?

"What do you know about taking care of babies?" he demanded, strengthening his resolve.

"I've read several books on the subject, I took a course in baby care a few years ago and I've been taking care of Bonnie for most of the day." It sounded like woefully inadequate experience even to her own ears, and she died a little inside when she saw Travis's scornful expression.

She could read his answer in his eyes. But before he could voice it, help came from an unexpected direction.

Jenny moved up to stand at her side. "Andrea is very good with Bonnie, Travis. She's someone I feel I can get along with and trust. Someone who's going to make my life easier instead of disrupting it. And I know she cares for Bonnie."

"She didn't even know that baby existed until two days ago!" Travis sputtered indignantly, surprised that Jenny had come to Andrea's defense.

Maggie moved up on Andrea's other side, her own baby in her arms. Her words were for Travis, but her glance strayed to her husband while she spoke. "How long does it take to learn to love someone?"

Somehow, Travis found his gaze locked with Andrea's, and, unbidden, he thought back to when he'd first met her. Her purse had been snatched as she was going into a department store, and he'd caught the perpetrator in the act. Andrea had been shaken, but determined not to let it show. She'd been cultured and gracious. She'd radiated class. She'd been everything he'd ever wanted but never knew he wanted until then. He'd longed to cherish her, to keep her safe. He'd fallen in lust, and he'd fallen in love. But he hadn't stopped to think that there was only one possible thing a woman like Andrea could see in a man like him.

Jenny's voice interrupted his thoughts, bringing him back to reality with a jolt. "Listen up, Travis. I agreed that Bonnie could stay with Rob and me because Lissa was my friend, and I loved her. And because I know you're still not well. I'm glad to try to help. But the baby-sitter I hired changed her mind. Maggie has her own children to take care of, and I have a full-time job. If you're not willing to let Andrea stay for two weeks while I look for another baby-sitter, you're going to end up taking care of Bonnie yourself."

Travis stared up at the three women who were standing shoulder to shoulder at the foot of his bed, looking as formidable as any army—an army that for some reason was hell-bent on overrunning his defenses. He assessed the situation and knew there was no way he was going to win this one. And he told himself that it wasn't important. Andrea wouldn't last two weeks. The novelty of playing nanny would wear off, just like the novelty of playing middle-class housewife had worn off after two years of being married to him.

"All right," he said, his voice tight with anger. "Have it your way. But at the end of two weeks, I give Andrea my decision, and she's out of here—no reprieves, no complaints."

Andrea felt a cold knot of fear form in the pit of her stomach. Could she stay with Bonnie for two weeks and then, if worse came to worse, leave her? But if she didn't agree, she'd be giving up the only chance she had. Her breath came out in a soft sigh. "Agreed."

"And one more thing. You're here to take care of the baby. Just the baby. Stay the hell away from me."

Andrea turned and left the room, unsure whether she had won or just prolonged an inevitable defeat. When she came to a stop, she was in front of the kitchen window, gazing out at a pitch-dark night unrelieved by any city lights.

Travis's words had hurt her—much more than she had thought he could ever hurt her again. She told herself it didn't matter. Nothing mattered except the fact that she'd just been given two weeks to chisel away at that barrier of resentment he'd erected between them. Two weeks to show him that he was wrong about her.

She heard footsteps and turned her head to look into Maggie's green eyes. "Are you all right?"

Andrea nodded as Jenny came up behind the other woman.

Caught with her guard down, Andrea instinctively tried to regroup and raise her defenses. Then Jenny reached out to squeeze her hand, and she was lost.

For once, she didn't want to hide her feelings. She sensed that she could trust these women, that they were genuinely concerned about her—even if she was almost a stranger to them. It was as if they all shared a kindred need for family and friendship that cut across social classes and geographic boundaries. It was a kinship that Andrea had never felt before.

"I'm sorry if I came between you and Travis," she said awkwardly, addressing both women. "But I'm not sorry that you stood up for me in there. I didn't expect it."

"Like I said," Jenny responded, "I know you care for Bonnie. And I also happen to think that you're just what Travis and that baby need."

It took a second for Andrea to absorb Jenny's meaning, then she shook her head. "There's no chance of Travis and me getting back together. When we were married, we couldn't communicate, and that certainly hasn't changed."

Jenny's eyes seemed to twinkle. "Well, he wasn't exactly warm and welcoming, but at least since you came he's not moping around like he'd died himself." Her expression grew serious. "And, if you'll forgive me for saying this, Andrea, I also had another motivation for having you stay—besides the fact that I really need your help. The truth is, I'm hoping that if Travis doesn't agree to let you have Bonnie, he'll wake up and realize he wants to keep her for himself and be a real father to her."

Andrea felt a little jab of apprehension at the mention of that possibility, but she nodded. "I understand. And thank you—" she looked at Maggie, including her in the acknowledgment "—thank you both for your support."

"We women have to stick together," Maggie told her. "And, listen, if you have any questions about how to take care of the baby, you just call me at the Double Diamond. I feel like I've become an expert on babies in the last few months!"

They all worked together to get coffee brewed and snacks laid out on the table, and Andrea relished the feeling of companionship that came from sharing the simple domestic chores. As unlikely as it seemed, she felt that she'd finally found a place where she belonged.

When the men left Travis dozing in the bedroom and came out to join their wives and children, the feeling of family warmth that Andrea had sensed before only increased. They all sat around the dining room table drinking coffee and snacking on homemade chocolate-chip cookies. They talked about horses, babies and cattle, and the things that had happened with the dudes that day.

Jude took a sip of coffee and leaned back in his chair. "I was damned glad to pack 'em all up and let the hands take them out on that hayride tonight."

Rob smiled at his brother's sour expression. "Most of them are real nice people. Don't you enjoy talking to them about what they do for a living and what things are like where they come from?"

"No."

Everyone laughed at Jude's curt response, and Rob explained to Andrea. "You'll have to excuse my brother. He's just a little, what you might call, anti-social."

Jude gave him a look that could have frozen sunshine. "Over the years, I've had to put up with so much from you, little brother, that it just naturally soured me on the rest of mankind."

Andrea stared at him, trying to decide if he was serious or not. Then he gave her a wink and a smile that made her realize just what Maggie saw in him. "It's been a real trial having a brother like Rob."

When Bonnie woke up, Andrea brought her out to show the visitors, her pride in the baby maternal. She found herself wishing that Travis could see how his friends fussed over his daughter, how the baby gurgled and cooed in response.

Despite her anger, her heart had gone out to him when young Todd had mentioned Lissa's death. She'd held her breath, unused to the open emotions being displayed. But, for once, Travis hadn't closed himself off. He'd been wonderful with Todd. If he would only let himself care about Bonnie, he'd be a great father. But just where would that leave her?

It was getting late when Jenny and Rob stepped outside to see the Double Diamond branch of the Emory brood off.

Andrea went to put a sleeping Bonnie into her crib.

She'd just put the baby down when there was a resounding crash from the direction of Travis's room. A bolt of terror shot through her, and she ran across the hall, scenes of blood and mayhem flashing through her mind. But even as she reached the doorway, Travis was rising from the floor, using the chair he'd apparently tipped over to push to his feet.

Totally forgetting the hostility that had passed between them earlier, Andrea rushed to his side and slipped an arm under his uninjured shoulder.

"I told you I didn't want your help," he growled. But despite his words, he leaned on her heavily as she assisted him back to bed. He half fell across the mattress, and Andrea drew the covers up over him.

"Where were you going?" she asked.

"I was returning from the bathroom," Travis admitted, even his voice sounding tired.

"You didn't have to walk all that way. For next time, I'll go get you a—"

"No, you won't!" Travis snapped. "I had enough of those things in that damned hospital."

"Then I'll get you a cane."

He brooded in silence for a moment before he responded. "If that's the choice I have, then I'll take the cane."

She had turned to leave when he said her name.

"Yes?"

"Will you give me my gun?"

Their gazes locked, and Andrea knew he wouldn't tell her anything about the shootings, or why he felt the need to keep a gun at his side in a house filled with friends. He wouldn't tell her that he felt helpless and defenseless, and that he couldn't rest peacefully until that situation was remedied. But then he didn't need to tell her that.

Reluctantly, she crossed to the bedroom closet and found his gun and the clipful of bullets that went with it. She had always hated even the idea of firearms, a hatred that had grown even more pronounced after the Chicago shooting. Now, she forced herself to pick up the weapon, and, holding it as if it might jump up and bite her at any moment, she walked to the bed and carefully handed both the gun and the clip to Travis.

He took them from her without a word, loaded the gun and put it under his pillow. He suddenly wanted to apologize for all the things he'd said to her earlier—even if many of them were true. He wanted to say he was sorry he'd been uncouth enough to deliberately try to humiliate her in front of his friends. He wanted to tell her that he had felt her pain and had hated himself for being the cause of it. Then he reminded himself that she had chosen to stay and plead her case. He didn't owe her anything, anything at all.

Except maybe one thing.

Andrea was halfway to the door when she heard him say distinctly, ''Thank you.''

She whirled to look at him, but he had closed his eyes and turned onto his side. She stood there for a moment, watching him, frightened by the fierce surge of protectiveness that welled up inside her. Suddenly she knew that there was more at risk here than who got custody of Bonnie.

If she weren't very, very careful, she could fall in love with this man again. And that, she knew from experience, was one story that did not have a happy ending.

Chapter Four

"Ohh...!"

Andrea jumped sideways, barely managing to avoid the scalding water that was sloshing over the rim of the saucepan she carried. Her sudden movement caused even more of the hot liquid to spill to the floor.

Taking a deep breath, she moved around the wet area on the linoleum and set the pan down carefully in the sink. Then she leaned against the counter, shoulders slumped.

From the direction of the nursery came another fretful whimper that signaled Bonnie would soon be fully awake, demanding her bottle.

Tears stung Andrea's eyelids, but she refused to let them fall.

Incompetent.

The word echoed accusingly in her mind. No Ballanger in memory had ever sunk low enough to merit that appellation, but that was clearly the word that described her now.

It had been a week since she'd arrived at Landon Ranch. A week that felt like a year.

Bonnie, who had seemed like the ideal baby, had turned into a colicky screamer who only slept for an hour at a time.

At first, Andrea had been terrified that Bonnie's condition was a result of something she was doing wrong. But Dr. Hooper had recommended a change of formula that appeared to be solving the problem. Now Bonnie was beginning to settle down and sleep for longer stretches, but a week of almost no rest had left Andrea an exhausted bundle of nerves.

On top of that, the ranch lacked some of the conveniences she had always taken for granted. There was no microwave and no clothes dryer here. Only an ancient, temperamental washer. And once the supply of disposable diapers from the hospital had been used up, she'd been left to cope with laundering cloth diapers and baby clothes as best she could. If she hadn't been afraid that Jenny and Rob would interpret it as an insult to their pride, she would have bought the appliances herself without a second thought.

And then there was Travis. Since Rob was busy with the dudes during the day and Jenny was occupied by her vet work, caring for Travis had fallen to Andrea. Lupe cooked breakfast and dinner, but the elderly Mexican woman promptly disappeared at the lunch hour. Andrea could hardly find the time to eat herself, but she had to prepare a nutritious lunch for Travis.

Not that he wanted or would ever admit he needed lunch or anything else from her. He avoided looking at her, barely spoke to her and generally made it obvious that he was counting the minutes until her two weeks were over and he wouldn't have to put up with her anymore.

But she'd known him too well not to sense the pain—both mental and physical—that he was in. He pushed himself relentlessly, eating every morsel of the food she served him despite the fact that he seemed to have little real appetite. He got up and walked a little farther each day, then went back to the bedroom, his face pale from the exertion.

And, though he'd long since abandoned the cane and his body was growing visibly stronger day by day, he remained just as withdrawn and grim as he'd been on her first night at the ranch. Often, she wondered how much longer she could stand to see him so bitter, to see how he was suffering. Maybe Jenny was right. Maybe Travis needed Bonnie in his life to help him get well emotionally and start living again. But if he decided to keep Bonnie, she would have to give the baby up.

Annoyed with the track her thoughts were taking, Andrea made an effort to concentrate on her own priorities. Travis was no longer hers to worry about, and she certainly didn't intend to push him to reconcile with his daughter if it meant she would lose Bonnie. He had succeeded in shutting her out completely, and from now on she would give him the same treatment. Travis Hunter would just have to heal himself!

She shook off the exhaustion that had her eyelids

slowly closing and reached up on top of the refrigerator for the roll of paper towels she needed to clean
up the spilled water. Despite her denials, she knew she
had to care about Travis for one very good reason: If
she didn't come to some kind of understanding with
him soon, if she didn't convince him that she could
be a good mother to Bonnie, she'd have to go back to
Chicago without the baby, without—

The barely audible sound of a shoeless foot sliding
against linoleum caused her to whirl around. She
should have been relieved when she saw that it was
only Travis entering the kitchen. Her heart should have
slowed its frantic beating, but it did not.

She remembered what he had told her once: "Most
people just don't expect a man as big as me to move
so quickly and so quietly. By the time they realize just
what they're up against, it's already too late."

Maybe she would have been better off if she'd
thought of that statement before making her own per-
sonal bargain with the devil. A devil who was wearing
low-slung jeans, and a white Western shirt that hung
loose and open against his chest.

Andrea's gaze was drawn inexorably to the long vee
of tanned skin that started at his collarbone and ended
where the hard muscles of his abdomen tapered down
and disappeared beneath the faded blue denim. She
found herself mentally filling in the details that were
hidden by the soft, snug cloth and felt the heat rush
to her face.

Quickly, she turned away from him, embarrassed by
her speculations and mentally railing against the surge
of excitement she was experiencing. She tried to dis-

tract herself by energetically wiping an already clean counter, but her thoughts raged on.

She didn't know why she was even bothering to try and hide her reaction. He was clearly oblivious to her existence. And here she was, her heart thumping like some giddy schoolgirl's. She resented herself for responding to him, and she resented him for eliciting that response.

But, by holding her goal of adopting Bonnie firmly in mind, she succeeded in keeping that resentment out of her voice. "What would you like for lunch today?"

Travis almost flinched at the sound of Andrea's voice. Ever since the night she'd given him his gun, he'd made up his mind that he wasn't going to let himself be attracted to her—even if it was just a physical attraction. He'd had to all but ignore her to accomplish that goal. He'd answered her only in monosyllables, barely acknowledging her presence. He'd willed himself not to look in her direction—even when her back was turned.

But it had been harder than he'd expected to tune Andrea out. The smell of her perfume, the softness of her voice had still affected him, haunting both his waking hours and his dreams. He'd heard the late-night crying, and Andrea's endless rocking and off-key lullabies. And he'd heard her worried conversations with Jenny and Maggie about the baby's health. What he'd hoped to hear, but hadn't—even once—was a complaint.

He couldn't fault her care of the baby and he appreciated the help she'd given him—although he'd rather bite off his tongue than admit it.

"I'm not crippled," he told her grudgingly, his gaze studiously on the cupboard ahead of him as he walked across the kitchen. "I can make a sandwich or heat up a can of stew by myself."

His tone was neutral, but Andrea only heard a criticism of her lack of expertise in the kitchen. She felt her cheeks burn even hotter as she turned around to face him.

"I may not be a gourmet cook," she said, biting off each word, "but at least you didn't go hungry."

Travis heard the cool anger in her voice and barely restrained himself from looking up at her in surprise. "I wasn't commenting on your cooking," he said finally, concentrating firmly on the loaf of bread he was taking out of the bread box. "I was just letting you know that I can take care of myself."

Andrea felt the dull ache of a hurt that she didn't want to acknowledge. This was so like Travis. She had spent hours playing servant to him, trying to help him recuperate, and he didn't have even a word of gratitude to offer her. Well, from now on, he could sit and rot for all she cared. She wouldn't lift a finger to help him again.

She stepped forward, paper towel in hand, intending to wipe up the water she'd spilled and leave the kitchen as soon as possible. But, her eyes blurred from fatigue and the unshed tears that seemed to be ever-present lately, she misjudged the perimeters of the wet spot on the floor. Her foot slipped on the slick linoleum and she skidded forward with an involuntary shriek of alarm.

Travis whipped around to face her, his eyes search-

ing for the unknown danger that had caused Andrea's
outcry, his hand already halfway to the gun snugged
in the back waistband of his jeans.

But before he could take any action, Andrea
slammed into him, jamming him against the edge of
the kitchen counter. Pain radiated from his spine where
the heavy metal of his gun had been forced into the
small of his back, and from his barely healed shoulder,
which had absorbed most of the impact of Andrea's
fall.

He snarled out a string of curses that would have
made a vice sergeant blush, but his arms went around
Andrea, steadying her, supporting her. He felt the contact like an electric shock, carrying awareness of Andrea to every cell in his body.

For the first time in a week, he looked at her. And
what he saw astonished him. He had never known her
to be less than perfectly groomed. Her designer clothes
had always been tastefully coordinated, her hair and
nails immaculately kept, her makeup artfully applied.

The woman he held in his arms now wore an old
cotton shirt that was wrinkled and stained, and a pair
of worn blue jeans that weren't in much better shape.
And for once there was no scent of expensive perfume
to torment him. Andrea smelled of something different. Baby powder and…some kind of milk. Slightly
sour milk.

Her face bore no trace of makeup, and there was
actually a sprinkling of freckles on the formerly por-
celain skin across the bridge of her elegant nose. Her
hair had been pulled back into a makeshift ponytail
with several slightly shorter strands falling down into

her face. And her beautiful brown eyes were peering up at his through that silky obstruction like an ill-tempered sheepdog's.

Despite his pain, he felt the sides of his mouth begin to curl upward, and he had to fight to keep the expression from becoming an all-out grin.

"Do you find something amusing?" Andrea asked, her initial start of fear and embarrassment giving way to annoyance. Her voice was filled with the same regal, carefully modulated annoyance that had caused heads to roll in the royal courts of Europe in the not-so-distant past.

Travis wasn't intimidated. What he was, was... aroused. The only time he had ever managed to see Andrea anywhere near this disheveled and vulnerable was in bed. After he'd unpinned her hair, stripped off her silk negligee and kissed away that imported lipstick she was so fond of. After he'd broken down her inhibitions one by one...

Andrea saw the intense look in Travis's eyes and felt the change in the male body standing so close to her own. Her anger at him and her self-consciousness over how she must look in the old clothes she'd borrowed from Jenny faded. Those emotions were replaced by a surge of desire that left her knees feeling weak. She became intensely aware of the warmth of the hard-muscled, hair-dusted chest beneath her palms and barely restrained herself from running her hands under the thin material of his unbuttoned shirt.

Travis saw Andrea's eyes turn from winter cold to summer hot. That heat burned into him, spreading through his body as his gaze traveled downward to the lush curve of her mouth. He remembered the sweet taste of her lips under his, and he wanted to taste them again. To drink from that tender mouth until he finally had his fill.

He let one trembling hand slowly slide down from her waist to the soft, pliant denim that covered her bottom. He cupped that rounded flesh possessively and pulled her even closer to his aching need. Then he bent his head to claim her lips.

An angry wail caused him to freeze an inch away from his goal. The sound of the baby's hungry cry hit him like a pail of ice water, washing away his desire and the haze that had been clouding his brain.

He was still being a fool. A stupid fool. The baby! She'd do anything to get custody of the baby—even seduce a man she hadn't been able to stand being married to. He hated himself for his weakness, and he hated her for trying to exploit it. No way would she ever use him again.

Unbidden, memories of their marriage flashed through his mind. The hurt and the anger he'd never had the chance to voice welled up inside him, demanding release.

He pushed her away abruptly, ignoring the burning pain in his chest that wasn't entirely due to his bullet wound. "Why don't you just give it up?"

Unprepared for his action, Andrea stumbled backward and caught herself on the far counter. "Give what up?" she asked, disoriented by the sudden change in him.

"Give up playing the good little mother and go

home. Tell the truth, aren't midnight bottles and dirty diapers getting a little old by now?''

His rejection stung, but the fact that he was voicing her own doubts stung even more. ''No one enjoys staying up all night or doing tons of laundry,'' she told him evenly.

Retrieving the roll of paper towels from the floor where she'd dropped them earlier, she squatted to wipe up the water she'd spilled. And she concentrated on ignoring Travis, hoping he'd go away and leave her alone. Instead, she felt him move closer to her. His presence inspired none of the warmth that it had only moments ago.

''That's what you were thinking when I walked into the kitchen, wasn't it, Andrea? You'd like to get out of here—you'd like to run. You've just got too much pride to admit that the newness has worn off, that you were wrong about wanting her!''

Travis's challenge and the thought of losing Bonnie brought forth a surge of love and possessiveness that made Andrea shake inside. Suddenly, she realized with intense clarity that despite all the sleepless nights and all the hard work, she wanted Bonnie now more than ever.

''You're wrong,'' she told him, struggling to keep her voice level. ''I'll always want her and love her! I will be—I *am*—a good mother.''

''You're living in a fantasy world. You're not her mother and you never will be!''

Andrea continued to wipe the now-dry floor, trying with all her might to control her thoughts and her emotions. But it was a losing battle. Hurt, and petrified that he would never let her have Bonnie, she responded to the raw feelings roiling inside her and instinctively went on the attack.

She stood and flung the paper towels into the garbage then turned to face him, eyes blazing with emotion. "How can you talk to me about doubting my feelings for Bonnie when you won't even look at her? When you refuse to even say her name? What's the matter, Travis, are you afraid that saying it will make her real to you?"

Travis stood transfixed by the sight of her. He'd never seen Andrea with her feelings so openly displayed, apparently willing to fight him tooth and nail for a child that wasn't even hers. A child he could never let be his. Myriad emotions flashed through him: astonishment, admiration, jealousy. He suddenly realized that he was jealous of her claim on a baby he could never acknowledge. And he was jealous because she was willing to fight so fiercely for the child when she had rejected his own love without lifting a finger to try to save it.

They stood there bleeding from invisible wounds, each holding the other's gaze in silence while feelings too complex to name arced back and forth between them.

Then the kitchen door was pushed open and the spell that had bound them together was broken.

Rob and Jude inched their way into the house, carrying a large cardboard box between them.

"Careful, now," she heard Jude say. "Set 'er down easy."

Both men bent down and set the obviously heavy box on the linoleum with sighs of relief.

"What's this?" Andrea asked, forcing her thoughts away from the man who had touched her—had hurt her—more deeply than any other human being. The man who was still standing in the same room as she was, too close for comfort.

Apparently oblivious to the undercurrents of residual emotion surrounding him, Rob gave Andrea a knowing smile and tore open the top of the carton.

Andrea looked down at the brand-new automatic washer, and for a few seconds her apprehension over Bonnie and Travis faded into the background. She felt like falling to her knees and kissing Rob's hand in gratitude.

Rob pulled out his pocketknife and began slicing open the sides of the box. "There's a matching dryer out in the truck, too. Jenny and I were going to buy a set of these as soon as our baby was born. We weren't planning on Bonnie coming to stay with us. When we found out, we called right away, but it took over a week for the store to get the color Jenny wanted."

Andrea struggled to come up with an appropriate response, only to find she couldn't get the words past the lump in her throat.

Rob looked up at her with a frown. "What's the matter? Don't tell me this is still the wrong color or something."

Shaking her head, Andrea finally managed to answer him. "As far as I'm concerned, it's just perfect!"

It didn't even occur to her to wonder at the elation filling her at the sight of a simple machine that she could have bought a hundred times over without once giving a thought to the cost. The fact that it was something that she needed so badly made it priceless in her eyes.

Travis couldn't help but stare at her. His ex-wife, the Chicago socialite, was almost in tears over a damned washing machine. Was he wrong to doubt her sincerity? Maybe she had changed. She obviously wasn't going to give up and leave before the two weeks were up. Was it just stubborn pride or was it a real commitment?

With a grimace of annoyance, Travis tore his gaze away from Andrea. One by one, he carefully walled away the emotions she'd aroused in him. After all, he had no reason to care how she felt. If she got hurt, it wasn't his fault. He'd warned her from the start that staying around here wasn't going to make him change his mind about the baby.

Now that he could get around again, he'd thought about taking himself out of the situation, about leaving Landon Ranch and going back to the house in town. Yet, somehow, he couldn't seem to do it. He told himself that it was because he needed to keep an eye on Andrea, to see that she left for Chicago before he did. Otherwise, she'd find some way to get around Jenny and Rob, and end up taking the baby away with her. And he wasn't going to allow Andrea to love and leave his daughter the way she had left him.

When the two weeks were over, Andrea would be back in Chicago, he'd be on his way to do what he had to do, and the baby would be safe with Jenny and

Rob. Andrea would forget all about the child, just as she'd forgotten him.

An angry wail, louder than the last one, pulled Andrea's attention away from the kitchen appliance and from Travis. This time, Bonnie wasn't fooling around. She definitely wanted her lunch.

Excusing herself to Rob and Jude, she removed the bottle from the pan of hot water, tested the temperature of the milk on her wrist, then proceeded down the hallway toward the nursery.

But when she was finally seated in the rocking chair that she'd had moved to Bonnie's room, holding the little girl in her arms, Andrea looked into the baby's blue eyes and realized with a wrench of her heart that Travis wasn't so easily forgotten. She had only seven days left to convince him to let her take Bonnie back to Chicago with her, or she'd never see the baby again.

Her mouth set in a hard line, Andrea started the chair in motion with a push of her foot. Now that she'd realized how much she truly wanted Bonnie and how hurt she'd be if she had to give her up, she was more determined than ever to get through to Travis—in any way she could.

There were bright lights, other shoppers all around, and the sound of Lissa's laughter. Then she stopped laughing, and her hand tightened on his arm. He turned his head and saw the man in the old army fatigue jacket coming toward them. He watched as the man drew a .38-caliber handgun from underneath that jacket. He tried to push Lissa away, tried to reach for his own gun, but the other man was faster. He heard the dull pop-pop *of the silenced bullets and expected to feel the impact in his own body. But instead, it was Lissa who stumbled and fell, crashing into his side, knocking him to his knees.*

He somehow managed to catch her with his left arm as he yanked his gun free of his shoulder holster. But before he could level the weapon, he heard two more shots. This time he felt the burning pain in his chest, felt himself falling backward to the floor. Still, his vision blurring, he managed to get one clean shot off before the man was lost in the crowd of shoppers.

He pushed himself up to a sitting position by sheer force of will, cradling his unconscious wife in his arms, willing her to live. In shock and disbelief, he felt their baby move beneath his hand. He suddenly realized that both his wife and his unborn child were about to die, and it was all his fault. All his fault....

It was the sound of his own scream that woke Travis up. Whether that sound was in his dream or real, he didn't know. He only knew that it was all too real to him. The shooting, the scream and the nagging feeling that there was something he'd overlooked. Again.

He concentrated fiercely on recalling the details of his dream, the details of the shooting. But the harder he tried to recall them, the faster they seemed to slip away.

Finally admitting defeat, he opened his eyes to the darkened room. He was sitting up in bed, drenched in sweat, his chest a burning agony. But it was nothing compared to the anguish and rage that simmered in his soul.

"It will be finished," he promised himself in a whisper. "It will all be over soon."

He sat there in silence for a long time, willing his mind to go blank, his heart to slow, his body to relax. Even though he knew there was no hope of falling asleep again that night.

When he felt he could trust his legs to support him, he got out of bed and pulled on his jeans. It was times like these that he sorely missed the cigarettes that Lissa had nagged him into giving up almost a year before. But he refused to start smoking again. Not that he expected to be around long enough to die of lung cancer, but because sticking to his abstinence was a matter of pride and self-discipline.

He stepped out into the hallway, intending to go to the kitchen for a cold drink and the half-finished newspaper he'd left on the table there. But somehow the thought of self-discipline had brought Andrea to mind. And now the image of her as he'd seen her just that morning refused to go away.

Against his will, his gaze traveled to the half-open door of the nursery. His breath caught at what he saw in the soft glow of the night-light.

Andrea lay sprawled across the small, roll-away bed that she slept on. Even in sleep she appeared poised to get up. She'd thrown the covers off, and one long leg was dangling over the side of the bed to touch the floor. Her dark hair, cascading across the pillowcase, was tangled, wild, out of control. Her ruffled white nightgown—had she borrowed it from Jenny? he wondered, he'd never known Andrea to wear a cotton gown before—had ridden up and pooled around the

juncture of her thighs like whipped topping on vanilla
ice cream.

He caught himself licking his lips at the thought and
felt a surge of anger as he realized just how aroused
he was. He told himself he would turn away and walk
down the hall to the kitchen, then go straight back to
his room. A room that offered him nothing but nightly
visions of violence and death.

Longing for one stolen taste of warmth and life, he
padded with all-but-silent bare feet to the nursery door.
Slipping inside, he forced himself, through habit, to
avoid noticing the second occupant of the room, the
one sleeping so quietly in her crib. It wasn't easy for
him to do, but so far it had been possible. Why was
he finding it so impossible to ignore Andrea?

Standing over her, he watched the rise and fall of
her chest in the soft light. The mounds of her breasts
seemed to beckon to him, the darker circles of the
areolas and the thrust of her nipples barely visible
through the thin fabric. He ached with the need to lift
the hem of her gown and bare her soft skin. To slip
inside her and make love to her so gently that they
could both pretend she still slept, that it was nothing
but a dream.

And who was to say it wasn't?

Slowly, he fell to his knees on the floor beside her
bed, holding back a gasp as his jeans tightened across
his arousal. His whole body feeling swollen and rigid
with desire, he let his hands hover a fraction of an
inch above her skin—close enough to feel its beck-
oning heat. A millimeter at a time, he traced every
curve of her body without once touching her. Then,

lowering his head, he buried his face in the pile of ruffles at her thighs. The scent of her made him groan aloud.

Andrea shifted in her sleep, wrapped in a sensuous fantasy too delicious to dispel. "Travis," she whispered.

He followed his name to its source, and allowed himself one final liberty. Leaning over her, shaking with the effort of restraint, he traced the outline of her lips with his tongue and kissed her as lightly as a summer breeze.

Andrea reached up to put her arms around her lover, to draw him closer to her. But she embraced only empty air. She opened her eyes and saw that she was alone in the room. Frowning in annoyance and frustration, she wondered how a dream could seem so real. Then she drifted off to sleep again.

In the kitchen, Travis opened the refrigerator and took out a cold can of soda. Closing his eyes, he pressed the can against the hot skin at the center of his chest and moved it left, then right. He felt the small nipples hidden under the swirls of dark hair contract in response to the cold. Shivering slightly, he trailed the container slowly downward over flesh and tautly stretched denim.

It had been stupid to go into her room that way. Stupid to tempt fate and his own control. Now he had to admit to himself what he'd been trying to deny ever since his confrontation with Andrea in the kitchen this morning. What had almost happened between them before Rob and Jude's arrival hadn't been all her fault. She didn't have to try to seduce him. He was all too willing to cooperate and to play the seducer himself if necessary. It was going to be hell trying to resist her efforts to persuade him to give her the baby when he was so susceptible to her charms. And, when the time came, it was going to be hell telling her that she had to leave alone.

All he needed was a handful of days, time to grow strong enough to do what he had to do. And to accomplish that, he needed to be able to keep his feelings buried deep inside. But every time he saw Andrea, it was as if she were banging at his walled-away emotions with a sledgehammer.

Exhaling loudly, he lifted the rapidly warming can away from his body. Then he popped the top and drained the contents in one long gulp.

It was going to be a very long seven days.

Chapter Five

"Let me take that for you, ma'am."

Andrea decided that, with Bonnie on one shoulder and the laundry basket balanced precariously on the opposite hip, she didn't stand a chance in a tug-of-war. She relinquished the basket to the flirtatious young cowboy as graciously as she could and continued walking across the ranch yard toward the clothesline.

A week ago, in Chicago, she might have found him amusing. Now he was just one more obstacle to be dealt with so that she could get on with all the things she had to accomplish before Bonnie's next feeding.

At least she didn't have to play servant to Travis anymore. He'd made it quite clear that he could get along on his own. Andrea told herself that she should be grateful that her workload had been reduced. Instead, she felt strangely bereft at the thought that she no longer had any real occasion to seek him out.

She hadn't seen him since their argument in the kitchen yesterday morning—unless she counted that vividly erotic dream she'd had last night. At first, she had wondered if Travis could actually have come into her room, but then she'd dismissed the possibility. He was determined to ignore her, not seduce her.

"...ma'am?"

Andrea tugged her thoughts back to the man who was walking beside her. He'd just said something, but she had been so absorbed in her own thoughts that she hadn't heard him. "I'm afraid I didn't catch that."

He gave her a smile that was so sincere she was sure he must have practiced it in front of the mirror until he got it just right. "I said I don't think we've been introduced yet. I know your name's Andrea, and I'm Will, Will Tavers. I help run the Landon Ranch and the Double Diamond."

"Oh, an executive," Andrea said dryly, giving him the smile *she* had perfected at her mother's frequent and tedious dinner parties. She resisted the urge to tell him that the only thing she'd noticed him doing around the ranch so far was to lean against the corral fence and put the make on any female guest who happened to cross his path.

The twinkle in his eye told her that he'd caught the lack of sincerity in her remark. "Executive, huh?" He rolled the word around on his tongue as if considering its effect. "Sounds good to me."

They shared a genuine smile before Andrea came to a halt under the large branches of a tree that grew in the ranch yard. Following her directions, Will spread the blankets she'd brought with her on the grass in the shade of the tree. Then Andrea laid Bonnie down carefully on the soft bedding and watched as the baby began to move her arms and legs as if she were trying to catch the stray beams of sunlight filtering through the thick canopy of leaves.

Satisfied that Bonnie was safe and comfortable, Andrea walked ten feet away to where the clothesline had been strung between two poles. Will followed with the laundry basket.

"Thank you," she said, taking the basket from him and setting it on the ground.

But instead of excusing himself and leaving as Andrea had assumed he would, Will looked down into the basket and raised an eyebrow. "I was wondering why you were hanging out clothes after Rob installed that new dryer."

He plucked a pair of beige satin-and-lace panties from the small pile of wet clothes and held them up for inspection.

Struggling between outrage and amusement, Andrea held out her hand. "If you don't mind…"

Will grinned at her, making no move to return the panties. "You can trust me with these, sugar. I'm a man who understands that fine, delicate things have to be handled with care."

Andrea pulled her underwear out of his hand and opened her mouth to make it very clear that she wasn't interested in being handled by him in any fashion. But a voice much deeper than her own spoke first.

"Isn't it time for you to get back to work, Will?" Travis said. The words were mild, but their tone and the look in his eyes made it clear that he would brook no argument.

Will certainly didn't seem inclined to give him one. He touched his fingers to the brim of his Stetson, gave Andrea a quick wink, then ambled off to where he'd tied up his horse.

Andrea watched him ride out of the ranch yard, then turned toward Travis, determined to let him know how annoyed she was at his interference. When she saw that he was continuing his daily walk, moving away toward the outbuildings of the ranch without even pausing to say a word to her, she became even more annoyed.

"For future reference," she called after him, "I'd like you to know that I really don't need your help in dealing with amorous ranch hands. Especially one as harmless as that."

Travis had acted instinctively when he'd seen Will sniffing around Andrea. He hadn't stopped to think, to remember that he had no reason to get involved. In fact, he'd barely managed to prevent himself from overreacting and punching Will in his smirking face. Now he nearly groaned aloud at Andrea's assessment of the situation. He didn't want her to have to learn the hard way that the subtle, polite rebuffs that worked in her high-society crowd wouldn't always do the job around here.

Despite his resolve to avoid any further involvement, he turned around to face her. "Will Tavers, harmless? If you'd given him any more encouragement, he'd have had you for lunch!"

Andrea felt a flush of anger and hurt climb her

cheeks. Did Travis think she was that naive, or just that susceptible to any stranger's charms? She was still trying to come up with the proper retort when he turned and walked away from her again.

She glanced back toward the tree to check on Bonnie, who was still gurgling happily at the sunlight, then threw the panties she still held over the clothesline. She bent to retrieve a handful of clothespins and jammed one into place. The delicate material snagged, then tore under the mistreatment, but she hardly noticed. She moved down the line, bending, straightening, and mangling as she went.

She had never felt so frustrated in her life. Her time on the ranch was dwindling away, and Travis was more distant than ever. What could she say to change his mind? What could she do that she hadn't already done?

The sound of Bonnie's whimpering diverted her attention just as she ran out of helpless garments to abuse. She looked over at the baby who suddenly seemed as unhappy as Andrea felt. At least Bonnie's distress was easily remedied.

"Okay, sweetheart. Just a minute."

She jogged the short distance to the house to retrieve the bottle that she'd left on the kitchen table by the back door. When she turned around to start back toward the baby, she froze, the breath leaving her lungs in a rush.

Something had come out of the brush near the tree and was gliding slowly toward the crying baby. Something that looked very much like a rattlesnake.

Andrea's mind was swamped by a thousand

thoughts, none of which she seemed capable of processing. When she acted, it was on instinct alone. She took one step forward, then another. Then she was running. She had no idea what she would do once she reached her destination. She just knew that she had to keep the snake from hurting Bonnie.

Time slowed to a crawl. The pounding beat of her heart, the dull thud of her sneakered feet hitting the grass, the sound of her own breathing, shut out all other sensory input. She was sure she wouldn't get there in time, sure that she'd be a second too late.

Then her feet registered the fact that she was running across the blankets. She jerked to a stumbling halt a foot away from the snake.

It reared back and coiled in sudden alarm, the sound of its rattles confirming her guess and seeming to fill her world. She froze, consumed by an ancient, inborn terror of the reptile in front of her. She stared into its black, bottomless eyes and saw her own death reflected there. Yet, inside her, a resolve grew stronger and stronger. This creature would not get by her. She would block its path until it retreated or, if it struck, she would find a way to make sure it went no farther.

Then, all at once, the snake made its decision. Andrea saw its head begin to arc forward. And she threw herself toward it.

Suddenly, there were two loud popping sounds and miraculously the snake was knocked sideways, out of her path of descent. She landed belly down on the warm grass. She lay there stunned for several seconds, unable to comprehend what had happened—until her shoulders were grabbed from behind, and she was jerked to her feet.

She found herself facing Travis. With what little reasoning ability she had left, she thought that she had never seen anyone who fit the definition of rage so completely. His face was scarlet and the veins in his forehead were standing out. She was vaguely aware that he was shaking her back and forth and screaming at her.

"What in the hell did you think you were doing?"

"S-s-snake," she managed to stutter inanely.

He released her so abruptly that she nearly fell down again. "What were you going to do to it?" he shouted. "Hit it with that?"

Andrea looked down to see that she was still clutching the baby bottle in her hand. Coherent thought began to return to her little by little. "I thought if I threw myself on top of it, I could pin it down and keep it away from Bonnie."

Travis stared at her, his head spinning, his chest still heaving painfully from the flat-out run that had brought him close enough to save her. If he'd taken just a split second longer... "What if I'd been too far away when I heard you scream my name? You could have been dead by now!"

Andrea didn't even remember calling out to him. She shuddered at the idea of what she had almost done, what had almost happened. Then she realized that her whole body was trembling. Travis was still swearing and ranting on about stupid fools. And Bonnie...Bonnie was screaming louder than her father was.

Andrea walked the few feet back to the blanket, and unwilling to trust her shaking legs, she dropped to a sitting position before picking the baby up. Even then, she found it a struggle to hold the bottle steady enough for Bonnie to nurse.

Her mind was full of more self-censure than even Travis could manage to throw at her. She *had* been stupid to rush out there holding nothing but a bottle. A broom or even a stick could have helped her fend the snake off. Or she should have snatched Bonnie away instead of confronting the animal. But the time and the distance had seemed so short! Had the seconds she'd stood frozen by the back door, trying to decide what course to take, been the deciding factor? She would never know.

There was a sudden, all-enveloping feeling of warmth and she realized that Travis had lifted the half of the blanket that was unoccupied and drawn it up around her back and shoulders. He'd stopped shouting and she hadn't even noticed. But now the silence was like a balm.

She could feel Travis's chest against her back holding the blanket in place, the side of his face pressed into her hair. And she could feel him trembling, just as she was. Had firing his gun brought back memories of the shooting in the mall? Was she to have that on her conscience, too?

Suddenly, she didn't care. She was just glad he was here with her, holding her, keeping her warm. She wanted to close her eyes and pretend that he was still her husband, that Bonnie was their child, that this was just the first of many such intimate moments to come.

But reality intruded. Bonnie began to fidget and Andrea saw that the bottle was empty. She shifted the baby to her shoulder to burp her.

Travis immediately left the blanket and turned away from her again. But when she was ready to get up, he was at her side once more, helping her to her feet.

When Andrea came to the kitchen after laying a sleeping Bonnie down in her crib, she saw that Travis was already seated at the kitchen table. She paused on the threshold of the room, too unnerved by the events of the day to risk another confrontation. And there was no one else to serve as a buffer between them. Lupe was sleeping—her siesta apparently impervious even to the sound of gunfire and screams—and the Emorys were both out working. For all intents and purposes, she and Travis were alone.

She had started to ease away slowly when he looked up and saw her standing there. Then it was too late to retreat.

"Come in and sit down," he said, gesturing across the table toward an empty chair. "I made a fresh pot of coffee."

Andrea complied reluctantly, sensing a new absence of hostility on his part, but not trusting it to last. She didn't want to lose the hope that had risen up inside her as he'd draped the blanket around her to keep her warm.

Half the coffee in her cup was gone before he broke the tense silence. "I'm sorry, Andrea."

She looked up at him in surprise, to find that he was looking down at the table, avoiding her eyes.

"I'm sorry I got so angry at you this morning."

Andrea shook her head, negating his apology. "You were right, I didn't stop to think things through. I acted like an idiot."

He looked up at her then, his own surprise evident. "You didn't have time to think, only to act. And what you did took a lot of courage."

Eyes downcast, Andrea took another sip of coffee in an attempt to hide the effect his words had had on her. She felt a warm glow inside at his approval. And she felt a closeness to him, as if a wall has started to come down.

"Of course," he added, only half-jokingly, "if I had to choose between having courage and having a .38, I'd choose the gun every time. It's a helluva lot more effective."

Andrea grimaced, the subject of gun control being an old source of disagreement between them. "You know how I feel about guns. But I do realize that people in rural areas have different life-styles and different needs. I can see where a rifle could be needed for protection or survival. It's handguns that cause the real problems, and it's handguns that should be banned."

"Oh, sure. Take away the law-abiding citizen's right to arm himself for protection. Then the criminals, who don't give a damn for any law—let alone a gun-control law—can kill without opposition."

"Any law can be enforced if the people get behind it."

Travis snorted in derision, but he was half smiling. The rhythm of their argument was so familiar to him, it was like an old song whose words he knew by heart. A song he hadn't heard for far too long.

Andrea became aware of the fragile rapport stretching between them, and felt like holding her breath lest it suddenly shatter and disappear. To someone else, it might seem strange that an argument over gun control could bring them closer. But, sadly, it was the nearest they had ever come to real communication in their marriage as it was the one issue Andrea couldn't stop herself from debating.

Now, for the first time since seeing her ex-husband as Travis Hunter, she felt as though she might be able to talk to him about the past—and the future. She struggled to find the right words, and when she spoke, her voice was little louder than a whisper.

"Would you tell me, please, why Trey Morgan 'died'?"

Travis's smile disappeared and he drained the last of his coffee in one gulp. For a second, he had the irrational urge to continue to deny her an explanation, to continue to punish her for divorcing him. But after what had happened less than an hour ago, he found that his desire to hold on to his anger over the past was rapidly disappearing. This morning, he'd realized that he still cared for Andrea on more than just a physical level. That realization had come close to panicking him. Just how much he cared and in what way, he didn't want to consider right now. He did know that he didn't want to be angry at this woman anymore. He wanted what she wanted. An explanation, a healing.

Grudgingly, Travis began talking. "The guys in the

know on the Chicago police force suspected that a
mobster by the name of Tony Valente had ordered the
hit on my uncle, but there was no proof. So when I
told you that I was going undercover to investigate my
uncle's death, it wasn't the whole truth. What I was
doing was infiltrating the Chicago mob. Eventually, I
even became one of Tony Valente's bodyguards.''

Andrea's hands clenched around her coffee mug.
The Mafia. Another secret, another worry Travis had
''protected'' her from. Somehow, she managed to bury
her resentment. The past was the past. She couldn't
afford to jeopardize her tenuous rapport with Travis
by hurling accusations at him now.

Unaware of Andrea's inner struggle, Travis continued his explanation. ''Through me, the police managed to bug an apartment where Valente met with
other mob members. One man, Maury Romano,
bragged about murdering my uncle in front of me and
on tape. But before Valente admitted to ordering the
hit, I was recognized as a cop by a man who'd just
arrived. My fellow officers, who'd been waiting outside, rushed in and arrested everyone. Valente vowed
vengeance for what he considered my betrayal.''

''So Romano was arrested for the murder of your
uncle, but Valente went free,'' Andrea said, striving
to understand exactly what had happened.

''Despite that fact, I felt I had achieved some mea-
sure of justice. Romano, the man who had pulled the
trigger on my uncle, was in jail. I still had to testify
at his trial, but I could finally go home. When I got
there, I found out that you had left me and filed for
divorce.''

Andrea couldn't meet his eyes, but she could hear the banked anger in his voice. If she'd only realized what he was going through at the time, she might have acted differently. But he hadn't shared any of it with her.

"And you were shot only days after you testified at the trial, days after the divorce became final." She would never forget that moment. She'd been staying at her parents' house then, in a state of almost catatonic withdrawal. But she'd been alert enough to overhear two of the maids discussing her ex-husband being shot—and her mother forbidding them to tell her about it.

"Valente ordered the hit on you as well as the hit on your uncle?" she asked, wrenching her thoughts away from her own misfortunes.

Travis nodded. "I was severely wounded. As soon as I regained consciousness after surgery, I was approached with the idea of "dying" and starting a new life in Texas as Travis Hunter. I agreed because I had no family, no life left as Trey Morgan."

Travis stopped speaking, the effort of holding back emotions and accusations finally becoming too much for him. Taking his mug to the counter, he poured himself another cup of coffee.

Andrea finally let herself examine her feelings. Prior to today, Travis had told her little about his uncle's death except that he needed to be out of town a lot investigating it—which she now knew had been a lie to account for the days and nights he'd had to spend living a second life as Valente's bodyguard.

When she had asked him for details, he'd told her

that what he was doing was confidential, police business. She'd never imagined it had anything to do with organized crime. And she had been so depressed for so long after her hospitalization that she hadn't had much contact with the outside world, hadn't read any reports of the trial or watched the news.

Now she realized that Travis was still holding out on her. He hadn't once mentioned how he'd *felt* about the breakup of their marriage or any of the other events that had happened to him.

"More coffee?"

Andrea looked up to see the subject of her thoughts hovering over her, pot in hand. She nodded, bemoaning the way those oh-so-blue eyes could make her heart skip a beat, as he began to pour the hot liquid into her mug.

During their marriage, she had tried to communicate with him, then backed down when he'd resisted. She'd run away from his anger, refusing to argue with him. But she was stronger now, a woman, not an unsure girl. She was through running away.

"How did you meet Lissa?"

Travis threw her a startled look and narrowly avoided spilling coffee onto the table. Discovering such directness in a woman he remembered as wanting to avoid confrontation at all costs was unnerving. He walked around the table and returned the carafe to its resting place, giving himself a moment to think.

By the time he sat down again, he felt a bit more in control. Why shouldn't he tell her about Lissa? He had nothing to hide as far as that was concerned.

"When I arrived in Texas as Travis Hunter, I set

myself up in Houston as a private investigator. A couple of years later, a businessman there hired me to spy on Jack Keel, another businessman who was blackmailing him. My client didn't want to go to the police, so he hired me to get something on Keel so he could even the score. I carried out my assignment while 'working' as Keel's bodyguard, then quit at the first opportunity. But while I was on that case, I came to Layton City and met Lissa. After I stopped working for Keel, I took another local job so I could stay in the area temporarily and be with her. A few months later, she got pregnant and we were married. I moved my detective agency to San Antonio so she could be near her friends.''

Andrea stared at him in disbelief. His ''explanation'' had been nothing but a dry, lifeless recitation of facts that told her nothing of what she really wanted to know. And there was no way he would ever tell her—unless she asked outright. So she did just that. ''Did you love her?''

Travis looked at her and swallowed hard, once again caught off guard by her directness. He thought of refusing to answer, but then he decided that maybe it was time she understood how it was with him. ''I don't think the kind of love you're talking about exists for me anymore,'' he said slowly. ''I loved her, and I wanted her and the baby. But I wasn't *in* love with her.''

He stopped talking, knowing he'd revealed more than he'd intended, and unwilling to compound the error.

Andrea had a series of reactions to Travis's revelation. She felt selfishly glad that he hadn't been in love with Lissa, and then almost immediately felt guilty for feeling that way. Then she realized he was implying that his first marriage had soured him on love. She wanted to tell him in no uncertain terms that she understood that, because it had had the very same effect on her. But she didn't. Because out of all that he'd said, she'd picked up another very important fact.

"You said you wanted Bonnie. What happened to change your mind?"

Travis felt his jaw tense. To hell with him and his feelings, it was back to the baby again! Well, that was one question he wasn't willing to answer. "I don't want to discuss that with you."

Aware that she had once again hit an invisible wall, Andrea felt disappointed and frustrated. "You're saying that you don't want to raise her, but you won't tell me why. And you refuse to let me have her even though I love her and want her. I don't think that's fair."

"I can see how you wouldn't." He looked at her, trying to decide how to explain himself. "I didn't think that you'd last through the diapers and the sleepless nights, but you did. What I saw today convinced me that you truly love her, that you're committed to her."

Andrea, pleased by his admission and puzzled by his continued opposition, tried to break in with a question, but he held up a hand to forestall her and kept talking.

"That doesn't change the fact that I don't want my daughter growing up in that phony high-society world

you'd be taking her back to. I want Lissa's friends,
Jenny and Rob, to raise Bonnie and teach her their
values.''

Andrea leaned forward, willing him to listen to her.
''Jenny and Rob's values *are* my values, Travis. Believe me, I hated the way I grew up, the hypocrisy,
the boarding school, the emphasis on the material
rather than the emotional. I don't intend to make the
same mistakes with Bonnie that my parents made with
me. I'm even willing to buy your house in Layton City
from you and bring Bonnie here every summer.''

Tears in her eyes, she reached across the table and
covered his hand with her own. ''If you ever cared for
me, Travis, and you truly don't want Bonnie, give her
to me. Jenny and Rob will have their own baby to take
care of soon. I have no one.''

Travis felt himself getting lost in those brown gold
eyes. He felt himself starting to waver, hovering on
the verge of granting her request. Then the thought
that he was that susceptible to her aroused both apprehension and anger, anger directed at himself. She'd
manipulated him into answering her questions, into revealing more than he had wanted her to know. But
he'd be damned if he'd let her manipulate him into
forgetting why she'd divorced him or changing his
mind about the baby! Maybe she was lying in order
to get the baby or maybe she even believed the things
she was saying. But he knew the kind of world she
came from, and he remembered the way she'd promised him forever and left him without even a goodbye
note.

He withdrew his hand from beneath hers and stood

up. "I'm sorry, Andrea. But like I told you before, I'm not changing my mind."

In a kind of numb daze, Andrea watched him open the back door and walk outside. Then, suddenly, she understood. He hadn't believed her! She'd bared her soul to him—she'd *begged* him—and he'd discounted everything she'd had to say. He was judging her just as everyone else always had, by her money and social class.

Well, she had no choice now. She'd have to set aside what remained of her pride. She'd have to go after him and tell him why she had divorced him and what had happened to her while he'd been undercover.

She started to get up, to act on her impulse. Then the second thoughts that had plagued her since the beginning made her hesitate. Consideration for Travis aside, was she doing the right thing? Had the things he'd said had any truth to them? If she took Bonnie away, would she be able to give the child the same love and positive experiences she'd get here with the Emorys?

Torn by indecision, Andrea lowered her head toward the table and let it rest on her crossed arms. In that moment, she came close to hating Travis Hunter.

Chapter Six

"What am I doing here?"

Jenny and Maggie exchanged what appeared to Andrea to be a guilty glance.

"Why, you're helping us with the Saturday-night party for the dudes," Maggie told her too innocently.

Andrea looked around the huge living room of Maggie and Jude's lovely Spanish-style ranch house. It was crowded with people, both neighbors and guests. Maids dressed in wide, colorful Mexican skirts wended their way through the crowd, dispensing drinks and hors d'oeuvres fresh from the cook's oven.

She let her gaze come to rest on Maggie and Jenny again and raised one eyebrow. "Exactly how am I helping you? There's nothing for me to do!"

Jenny gave her a smug look. "Exactly. Turnabout is fair play. You never let me help with Bonnie. Even on those nights when I did manage to crawl out of bed, you insisted on handling things yourself so that I could go back to sleep.''

Maggie nodded her agreement. ''And you've worked so hard the last week and a half taking care of Bonnie and Travis that we knew you needed to get out and enjoy yourself. You're not mad at us for fudging on the truth a little, are you? It was for a good cause.''

Andrea couldn't help but be touched by their concern. She had never really had friends to worry about her, only acquaintances who wanted to be seen in her company so that they could enhance their own positions in society.

She gave them a smile and smoothed the skirt of her blue designer dress with newly manicured hands. ''Thank you for going to the effort. That trip to the beauty parlor in Layton City really did wonders for my morale. And I really am enjoying myself.''

It wasn't far from the truth. She would have enjoyed the party if it hadn't been for the fact that she was worried sick about the situation with Bonnie. She was angry with Travis for refusing to believe that she could provide a good home for Bonnie. And she was angry with him for making her doubt herself, even temporarily.

Now she was more determined than ever to confront him and win Bonnie. And she had even figured out a way to do so without compromising her pride. She could talk to him about the reasons she'd decided to divorce him without revealing her secret. Maybe that would convince him that she wasn't as shallow as he believed—and that he wasn't entirely blameless.

Since she'd made her decision, she'd even been looking forward to the confrontation. But there was just one problem. Travis hadn't let himself be alone in the same room with her since the day of the incident with the snake. She'd had no further chance to try to win him over, and she only had four days left on the ranch.

"How are things going with Travis?" Jenny asked, right on cue.

Andrea took a sip of the cola she was holding, wishing it was something stronger. "He admits I'm doing a good job with Bonnie, but he won't agree to let me have her."

Both women made sympathetic noises.

"It's not an easy situation," Maggie said softly.

Jenny adjusted an earring. "If Lissa were here right now, she'd boot him in the butt."

The women looked at each other for a few seconds, then all three of them burst out laughing.

"I'm sorry," Jenny said after she'd caught her breath.

Andrea was still smiling. "I'm not offended. From what Travis has told me, Lissa was a wonderful woman and they really cared for each other."

"He was so good to her," Jenny said a little wistfully. "I never thought Lissa would get married again after Ted Shafer."

"An old boyfriend?" Maggie asked.

Jenny shook her head. "Worse. She actually married the jerk. He used to beat her black and blue. I finally talked her into leaving him. Only a few days later, he almost killed a man in a bar fight and was sent to Huntsville Prison. We all breathed a sigh of relief, I can tell you.''

''Lissa divorced him while he was in prison?'' Andrea wanted to know. When Jenny nodded, Andrea frowned, trying to fit it all together. ''That certainly doesn't sound like a woman who could kick Travis in the butt.''

''Once she got over Shafer, she was really mad at herself for letting him treat her that way. She went to San Antonio and signed up for one of those self-defense courses. Swore she'd never take any guff from any man again. And she sure didn't. At my wedding to Jack Keel, when Travis tried to stop Rob from stealing me away, Lissa flattened him.''

Andrea, who had been listening with interest up to that point almost choked on her soda. ''What did you say?''

Jenny's eyes seemed to light up at the memory. ''A man named Jack Keel was blackmailing me into marriage, and Rob came riding down the aisle and carried me off. Travis was working for Jack at the time so he was bound to try to stop Rob. Of course, I don't think Travis was trying his absolute best. None of us knew that then, though. Least of all Lissa.''

Andrea took another swallow of cola. A long one. ''How did all of you ever become friends?''

''Travis didn't like the things Jack was doing so he quit. Rob admired him for that and hired him to work as a ranch hand. After Travis married Lissa, they moved to San Antonio, and he opened a detective agency.''

There was a moment of silence as Andrea tried to

make sense of it all. Travis obviously hadn't told his friends anything about his past—in Chicago or in Texas. "How would Travis know anything about working on a ranch?" she asked, hardly realizing that she spoke aloud.

Maggie and Jenny both looked at her with the same slightly confused expression on their faces, but Jenny was the one who spoke. "He grew up on his father's ranch in New Mexico. Didn't he?"

Andrea felt as if her world had tilted slightly. Travis had told her that his parents were dead, nothing more. She'd never dreamed he'd lived on a ranch or that he'd ever been near New Mexico. She groped for a response to Jenny's question, and came up with the truth. "He never told me about that. I met him in Chicago."

Suddenly, she felt sick inside. Who was the real Travis Hunter? Had he had another life before Trey Morgan or had his childhood just been too painful to talk about? She had no way of knowing because he had never cared enough or trusted her enough to tell her. Now she'd been caught in his web of lies and half-truths, unable to confide in Maggie and Jenny because she didn't know if she'd be revealing things about Travis's past that might endanger him.

Only moments ago, she'd been part of a circle of caring friends. Now she felt like an outsider again, separated from the other two women by Travis's deceit.

"What are you three beautiful ladies looking so sad about? This is a party. Smile a little!"

Rob came up behind Jenny and kissed her neck until

she squirmed. Jude put one arm around the waist of a suddenly beaming Maggie. And Andrea couldn't help the feeling of pure envy that shot through her.

"I think I'll go check on the babies," she said, wanting an excuse to be alone.

"We did that five minutes ago," Maggie reminded her. "The music's about to start. Stay here and dance a little."

Rob smiled at her over Jenny's shoulder. "Jude and I might be persuaded to take you around the floor a time or two if you twist our arms."

"Thank you, but I..." Andrea lost her train of thought as she looked up at the front of the room and saw three musicians tuning up. A piano player, an accordionist and a guitar player. And the guitar player was Travis. Another thing about himself that he'd never bothered to mention to her.

Seeing her expression, Jenny and Maggie began to talk at once.

"Len usually plays the guitar at parties..."

"But he was sick..."

"So we asked Travis to sit in."

Andrea looked at them closely, but both women seemed to be avoiding her eyes. "Well, I'm glad you did," she told them.

"You are?" Jenny asked hopefully.

"Yes, I am. Because I have something I want to say to Mr. Travis Hunter."

Placing her empty glass on a passing tray, she began walking toward the front of the room.

"Well, so much for your matchmaking, Jen," she heard Rob say behind her. "I don't know what she's all het up about, but I'll betcha ten dollars ol' Trav ends up wearing that guitar.''

Travis looked up as she approached, then quickly averted his eyes when he recognized her. The action topped off Andrea's temper.

"I need to talk to you," she said, struggling to control her voice.

"I don't think we have anything left to say to each other."

"Well, I think we do."

Travis finally looked up and saw the barely leashed anger in her eyes. Whatever it was she wanted to say, it appeared that she was going to say it in public if he didn't respond very soon. Reluctantly, he put the guitar down on top of the piano and led the way out of the room.

Andrea followed him down a hallway, through a bedroom and out into the shadows of a dark patio. Only a few feet away, moonlight and outdoor lighting combined to turn the surface of a huge swimming pool into shimmering blue ice—a color that reminded her of Travis's eyes.

Ruthlessly, she cleared her head of the image and waited for him to turn and face her. But he remained as he was, not deigning to look at her. Her anger rose another notch.

"Still hiding, Travis? You can turn around. It's too dark out here for me to see your face. That *is* why you brought me out here, isn't it?"

Travis swung to face her, his own anger ignited. And he almost blurted out the truth. He hadn't wanted to be able to see *her*. The one glimpse he'd had of her tonight had all but taken his breath away.

"I brought you out here," he said, his voice rough, "because you wanted to talk to me. If you've changed your mind, we can go back inside."

"No, I haven't changed my mind. You just made a fool out of me with your lies. You probably just cost me the only real friends I've ever had!"

Travis frowned into the darkness. "What in the hell are you talking about?"

"Jenny and Maggie. You call them your friends, too. But you haven't told them anything about your life as Trey Morgan."

"The less they know about any of that, the safer it is for everyone."

"And you didn't even tell them you owned a detective agency in Houston or why you were really working for Jack Keel. What does that have to do with safety?"

"There was no need for them to know. The more people know about a person, the more they want to know."

"And you might actually end up having to reveal your true self."

The jibe hit too close to home. "How I live my life is my business!"

Andrea felt tears come to her eyes. "It was my business once, Travis. I was your wife, but you wouldn't let me share any part of you. That's why I divorced you. But until tonight, I never knew just how deep it ran. Tonight, I realized that I never knew you at all. It took Jenny to tell me that you grew up on a ranch in New Mexico. Or is that a lie, too? Do you even know what the truth is anymore?''

She gasped as Travis stepped close and grabbed her arm. His face was in shadow, but she could feel the anger in every line of his body. ''The truth, Andrea, is that you've got four more days left. And I'm counting the minutes.''

She stumbled slightly as he released her and stood there stiffly as he walked back inside, leaving her alone in the darkness.

''Have you seen Andrea?''

Rob looked up from the full plate of buffet food he was balancing on his knee and shook his head. ''Not for an hour or more. But then it is kinda crowded in here.''

Travis made his way by the people seated around the edges of the room, looking for a glimpse of blue.

After he'd stumbled through the first two tunes, Len, the ''sick'' guitar player, had made a miraculous recovery and had shown up to reclaim his abused instrument. Travis had ended up on the fringes of the crowd, nursing a beer and thinking over what had happened earlier.

He had been angry at Andrea to begin with because she made him ache with wanting her just by being near him. He had reacted to her attack on him instinctively, her anger making his burn even hotter. And then the things she'd said had put him on the defensive. Probably, he realized now, because they were true.

He had always been a loner, withdrawn, secretive,

wary of exposing himself unnecessarily. It had served him well as a policeman and a private detective, but had it somehow caused the breakup of his marriage?

He'd tried to think back to what it had been like when he was married to Andrea. But all he could remember was that things had been fine between them one day, and then he'd come home a couple of weeks later to find she'd left him.

Had something been going on that he hadn't been aware of, or was this just some strategy Andrea had come up with to convince him to give her the baby? Now that he had time to think about it, he'd decided that he wanted to know the answer.

Travis finally caught sight of his quarry on the periphery of the dance area, near the buffet tables. She was dancing, and his jaw tightened when he saw who her partner was. Rob had pointed the man out to him a few days before as the most illustrious guest ever to stay at the dude ranch. Senator Trenton D. McGuire. Leave it to Andrea to gravitate to the richest, most successful man in the room.

Andrea gave the senator her best social smile and nodded her head in agreement to whatever it was he'd just said. He was a brilliant conversationalist with only one subject in his repertoire: himself. She had tried to divert him with questions about the Texas political scene, but his answers were so slick and uninformative that she soon let him lapse into his favorite topic. She was sure she would have been asleep long ago if it hadn't been for the fact that she had to keep her feet moving. To think she'd come all this way only to get stuck with a man who would have fit right in at one of her mother's dinner parties!

For the hundredth time, she mentally replayed every word of the conversation she'd had with Travis by the pool, and once again she wondered how she could have been so stupid. In the span of a few minutes, she had let her anger alienate him completely and destroy what might have been the last chance she had to win him over. The last...

She gave a small gasp of surprise when the subject of her thoughts appeared, looming over the senator's well-padded shoulder. From the expression on his face, it didn't appear that his mood had improved since their last encounter.

"I thought you were supposed to be baby-sitting, Andrea, not entertaining the guests."

The senator turned and peered up at Travis through the thick lenses of his glasses. "Are you speaking to this lady, sir?"

"Yes, I am. And if you don't mind, I'd like to speak to her some more. Alone."

Travis tried to move past the other man, but the senator's portly body had suddenly become a brick wall.

"Perhaps, sir, you should go to the kitchen and get some black coffee."

"And perhaps, you stuffed shirt, you should mind your own business!"

Andrea, whose verbal protests had been drowned out by the music and the deeper voices of the two men, stepped forward, determined to intervene before things went any further.

Travis put a hand against the older man's arm and pushed in an attempt to move him aside. It had the desired effect—and then some.

The senator stumbled sideways, tripped over Andrea's foot and made a ten-point dive, face first into a huge double chocolate cake in the center of the endmost buffet table. The table collapsed under his not inconsiderable weight, causing a chain reaction. One after the other, the five buffet tables fell to the floor, spewing punch and edibles halfway across the room.

There were screeches of surprise and angry curses, and everyone turned to look at the spectacle of a Texas senator covered with chocolate cake, apple cobbler and lemon meringue pie trying unsuccessfully to struggle to his feet.

A half-drunk Will Tavers gave a piercing whistle and lifted his glass in salute. "Give the old windbag another one for me, Travis!"

Chapter Seven

"Want me to freshen your coffee?"

Andrea looked up from her seat at the kitchen table and shook her head.

Jenny filled her own cup and pulled out a chair. "You know it's been three days since the party, and I've been so busy with sick animals—not to mention hung over ranch hands—that I haven't had the chance to talk to you once."

Andrea gave her a glum smile. "Frankly, I've been trying to avoid you. After what happened at the party, I'm surprised you'd want to talk to me at all. I feel like a fool."

"Men have been making fools out of women and blaming it on them since Adam and Eve. You're not alone."

Andrea gave her a grateful look. "But what about the senator? I called to apologize, but I'm sure Maggie and Jude are going to lose business over this. If there's any way I could make it up to them…''

"Don't worry about it. We assured the senator that his stay with us would be free. Travis apologized for his 'drunken' behavior. And we got everyone we know to call or come by and tell Senator McGuire how gallant and brave he was, what a good sport he was, and how they'd be sure to vote for him in the next election. By the time we were finished, he was thinking of his dive into the cake as a shrewd campaign move.''

Andrea joined in Jenny's laughter. "The poor man! He was a sight, wasn't he?''

When the laughter had run its course, Andrea continued in a more serious vein. "Thank you for being so understanding, Jenny. And thank you for accepting me the way you have, you and Maggie. You've both made me feel as if I belong here.''

Jenny took a sip of coffee and nodded. "We know all about the need to be accepted, Maggie and I. Before she came here, she was always judged by her looks and treated like some scheming sex kitten though she's the sweetest, most generous person I've ever met. And I thought of myself as a homely little bookworm, so insecure that I couldn't believe that Rob could really be in love with me.''

"And I've always been judged by my family and my social position when all I ever wanted was someone to accept me for myself. Someone to…'' She paused, suddenly feeling too exposed.

"Someone to love you? That's what most everyone

wants in one form or another. That's why you really followed Travis out here, isn't it? You still love him.''

Andrea opened her mouth to deny Jenny's statement. Then she realized that it was true. She *was* still in love with Travis. She'd known that for a long time. She just hadn't wanted to admit it to herself. She'd come running after him as soon as she'd seen the newspaper clipping, long before she even knew a baby existed. That was one of the reasons she wanted Bonnie so badly—Bonnie was *his* child. And it was the real reason she hadn't wanted to go all-out in fighting him for the baby.

The phone rang, breaking into Andrea's thoughts. Jenny got up to answer it. When she hung up, she was already reaching for her medical bag and her Jeep keys.

''Sorry to cut this short,'' she told Andrea as she headed for the door, ''but I've got an emergency. Take all those packages of chicken out of the freezer for me, would you? Lupe called in sick today, so I have to cook dinner for everyone tonight. We'll finish our talk later, I promise.''

Andrea sat at the table long after her friend had left, fingering her empty coffee cup and thinking. She had finally faced the truth, and she didn't like what she saw. She loved Travis *and* Bonnie, and she was probably going to lose them both.

Travis was almost completely recovered now. Dr. Hooper had visited, removed the bandage and pronounced him one lucky devil and the worst patient he'd ever had.

He would be going off on his own soon, back to

San Antonio, or maybe somewhere else. And she'd be leaving, too. Tomorrow was her last day on the ranch.

And whatever it was that Travis had wanted to talk to her about the night of the party, he hadn't mentioned it since. In fact, she was sure he'd been purposely avoiding her.

There was only one card she had left to play. If she played it, she might win Bonnie, but it would only be because Travis pitied her and felt responsible for her pain. And if she took Bonnie that way, she'd surely be leaving Travis more bitter, more withdrawn and feeling even worse about himself than he did right now. She loved Bonnie, but could she bring herself to walk over Travis to get her?

If only she and Travis could forgive each other for the past, then maybe they could start a new life together, with Bonnie. Yet she knew that was just a dream. She might love him, deep down he might even still care for her, but they could never make a relationship work. They had been incompatible to begin with. Even if she had once been naive enough to believe a baby could solve that problem, she didn't believe it now.

But then, wasn't she being naive to believe that Bonnie could help Travis deal with his grief and become part of life again? If she gave Bonnie up, Travis might just continue to ignore the child. She knew that there was only one way to find out. They were alone in the house. There would be no better opportunity.

Minutes later, Andrea stood over Bonnie's crib, warm bottle in hand. The baby was moving restlessly, on the verge of waking. She had only seconds to make her decision.

She tried to imagine her life without the baby and realized that what she'd once thought of as contentment had only been numbness. How could she go back to that? Even for Travis?

Tears welled up in her eyes and, before she could prevent it, one had fallen onto the baby's face.

Bonnie responded with a full-throated wail, and Andrea made her decision. Quickly, before she could change her mind, she ran out of the room.

The sound of crying followed her through the living room to the kitchen. She stopped long enough to scribble a note and set the bottle beside it. Then after retrieving her purse and keys, she ran out the front door and down the steps to her car.

Tears blurring her vision, she managed to negotiate the long driveway and pull the vehicle up behind the shelter of a huge oak tree. She shut off the engine and let the sobs rack her body. And she cried until she couldn't cry anymore.

Travis had been waiting for Andrea to approach him and try to talk to him again. He'd been waiting for three days. He could have gone to her, of course. But if he waited for her to make the next move, it gave him the advantage, and it allowed him to save face— something he'd been feeling a little short of after that fiasco at the party.

He knew she'd come to him today. She had to. Tomorrow was the end of the two weeks. *And what if you're wrong, smart guy?* an inner voice demanded.

Then, he told himself, it was just as well. It wasn't as if he was hoping for some kind of reconciliation. The past was past, and he had no future left to share with anyone, anyway.

But it would have been nice to hear what she had to say. To see her one more time. To touch her face....

He sat up on the side of his bed, disgusted with himself. The woman had walked out on him without a word, and he was having romantic fantasies about her! The episode at the party apparently hadn't been enough to convince him she was bad news.

A sound crept into his consciousness. A repetitious, annoying sound. After a second, he realized that it was the baby crying. Andrea would soon come running, just as she always did. Maybe he should open his door and meet her in the hallway. Accidentally, of course.

He listened for her footsteps, but they never came. And the crying went on.

Something was wrong. Andrea would never let the baby cry this long.

Cold with apprehension, he swung to his feet, tucked his gun in his back waistband and flung open the bedroom door.

"Andrea?" he called loudly.

The house seemed to echo with his shout. But no one answered. Where the hell was she? Not in the nursery.

His hand on his gun, he moved through the other rooms one by one and looked out the front living room window. Her things were here, but her car was gone. What was going on?

Then he reached the kitchen and found a note and

a bottle. The note read: "I had to go out. Please feed the baby for me."

"Is she kidding?" Travis said aloud. The empty room held no further answers.

"She must have left this for Jenny," he muttered. But Jenny wasn't here. Now what was he supposed to do?

He stared at the bottle for a long moment, listening to the bone-jarring crying. And knew he had no other choice.

Like a condemned prisoner, he walked up the hallway to the nursery. Maybe, if he was lucky...

He pointed the bottle down into the crib in the general location of—a quick glance assured him—the baby's head. But the crying continued unabated.

Finally, Travis was forced to conduct a more thorough assessment of the situation. He looked down into the crib. Everything was lined up right, but the baby was turning its head away from the bottle.

She was shrieking louder than ever, face red, arms and legs flailing, the perfect picture of outrage.

Cursing, he put the bottle down and reached into the crib. He couldn't recall ever picking up a baby before, but he did have vague memories of a police academy lecture on how to deliver one. "Support the head, support the back..."

Somehow he managed to get the squirming bundle of temper installed in the crook of his arm. And after an initial refusal, she accepted the bottle, still snuffling and giving an occasional whimper of displeasure. Then her gaze fixed on his face.

He really looked at her then. He couldn't help it.

And what he saw broke his heart. She had his eyes and her mother's hair.

Feeling suddenly weak, Travis sank onto Andrea's bed, still holding the baby. Memories come flooding into his consciousness, the hopes and dreams about babies and the future he'd once shared with Andrea all tangled up with the similar hopes and dreams he'd shared with Lissa.

Holding their child in his arms, he found that he could no longer keep the pain of Lissa's death at bay. He sat there on the bed, cradling his daughter and crying like a baby, himself.

When he was finally able to regain control of himself, he felt drained of grief, but he was angry. Angry at Andrea for making his daughter real to him when he had no future to spend with her. Now it would only be harder for him to leave her. Had Andrea done this to him on purpose? If so, why? What would she have to gain from it?

But there was only one person in the room who might know the answers, and she was too young to talk.

Andrea crept back into the house and entered the nursery as quietly as she could. Travis was lying on his side on her bed with Bonnie asleep in the circle of his arm. His eyes were closed and there were what looked like dried tear tracks on his face. Her plan had worked then. She wasn't sure whether to mourn or rejoice.

She walked to the bed, set the empty bottle aside, and carefully picked up the baby. As she lowered Bonnie into the crib, it occurred to her that this was the last time she'd be holding her. But she didn't cry. She had no tears left to shed.

As quietly as she could, she gathered up the few possessions she'd had occasion to use and packed them. Then, trying not to think about the finality of what she was doing, she picked up her suitcase and overnight bag and walked out into the hallway.

Before she could take two steps, she was grabbed from behind and propelled through the open doorway of Travis's bedroom. She dropped both bags and whirled to face her attacker.

The sight of Travis glaring at her was almost a relief.

"Sneaking away again? I seem to remember that's your specialty."

"We had a bargain. It's time for me to leave."

"Not before you explain what went on here today. You left me alone with Bonnie on purpose. Why?"

Andrea sank onto the edge of the bed, knowing she wasn't going anywhere until she told him what he wanted to know. "I wanted you to bond with the baby because you need Bonnie, and she needs you."

"Who asked you to interfere, Dr. Fix-it? You have no idea what you've done!" He turned and pinned her with a stare that had caused hardened criminals to quail. "Besides, I thought *you* wanted the baby."

Andrea looked down at her hands. "I do. But I think you two need each other more."

"And why should you care what I need?"

Andrea sighed, wishing he would just let her leave

without putting her through this humiliation first. "Because I...care about you."

"You care about me?" Travis stepped closer to her, suddenly feeling he had to catch every word. "Is that why you divorced me?"

"It's a long story," Andrea said evasively.

She felt the bed dip as Travis sat down beside her. "I've got all night."

Knowing she was trapped, Andrea tried to get it over with as quickly as possible. Avoiding his eyes, she forced herself to speak. "While you were undercover, I found out that I was pregnant."

She heard his indrawn breath, felt his astonishment, but she plunged ahead, wanting to get it all said before her courage failed her. "Not long after I found out, I was trying to reach something in a high cupboard and I fell. I...was knocked unconscious, and I had a miscarriage at home all alone. When I finally came to and called 911, I was rushed to the hospital. They...they had to remove my uterus to stop the bleeding."

Travis was stunned by the pain she'd just inflicted on him with those few words, stunned by the pain she'd had to endure alone. He'd never imagined anything like this! If only he'd been there, maybe...

"Why didn't you call my number at the police department and explain what was happening? They would have gotten in touch with me as soon as they could. They would have sent someone to be with you so you wouldn't be alone."

Andrea wondered how she could explain the way she'd felt then. The rage, the emptiness, the despair. The need to blame someone. "The hospital wanted to call you, but I asked them to contact my father, instead. At that point, you'd been away for almost two weeks. I felt that if you had been home with me, things might have turned out differently. I blamed you for what had happened to me. I was very angry and very depressed.

"My father came to get me from the hospital, and he had his lawyer file the divorce papers. At the time, I thought that's what I wanted. I sat in my old room in my parents' house, reading, brooding, staring into space. The only time I showed any real interest in anything was when I heard the maids talking about how you'd been shot. I called the hospital they'd taken you to, and I was told that you were dead."

Travis wanted to reach out to her, wanted to take her hand, but he was afraid she'd push him away. So he watched her as she continued talking, her face a stark white oval framed by dark hair.

"It was a year before I started to get my life back together again, before I went back to school to get my master's degree. And during that year, I made a solemn promise to myself. That I would speak up and confront people when it mattered. That I wouldn't be afraid to admit how I felt to others and to myself. I started with my parents. I told them that if they wished me to remain their daughter in more than just name, they would have to respect my right to be different from what they believed I should be. They agreed, somewhat reluctantly, but they agreed. We'll never be close, but we've reached an understanding."

They sat in silence for a moment before Travis found the courage to speak. "It won't make any difference now, but I'd like to tell you why I felt I had to go undercover, to catch Valente.''

When she didn't object, he continued talking. ''I did grow up on a ranch in New Mexico. My mother ran off with some rodeo cowboy when I was five. My father had a dab of Welsh and Scots, a little Apache and a whole lot of Irish. In him, it wasn't a good mix. He finally managed to finish drinking himself to death when I was fifteen, and the bank took the ranch. The state located my mother's brother in Chicago and that's how I came to live with Uncle Fred. For the first time, I had someone to look up to and love. That's why I felt so strongly that I had to avenge him.''

He sighed deeply, feeling inadequate. He hadn't had much practice at putting his feelings into words. ''I guess what I'm trying to say is, I wasn't away because I didn't want to be with you, Andrea. After the guy who pulled the trigger on my uncle was arrested and I came home, I almost went crazy when I found you gone. There wasn't even a note. I got so desperate I finally called your father. He told me that you'd decided to file for divorce and that all further communication would be through our lawyers.''

''He never told me that you'd called.''

Travis made a derisive sound. ''Now why doesn't that surprise me? When I found out that you were living with your parents, I thought you hadn't really cared for me at all. That you'd just been playing at being a middle-class housewife. Then, when it wasn't fun anymore, you'd gone running back to your life of luxury. I told myself that it was for the best—that that was where you were meant to be. But somehow…that didn't stop the hurting.''

Andrea was touched by an admission she knew had been very difficult for him to make. She tried to help him by putting the rest of his story into words. "So when you were shot and offered a new life as Travis Hunter, there was nothing to stand in your way, no reason to try to say goodbye.''

She thought about all the pain they had each unintentionally caused the other and she felt a deep sense of loss. "Why, Travis? Why was our marriage so unhappy? Why wouldn't you talk to me about how you felt then, instead of now, when it's too late?''

"Unhappy?'' Travis turned to look at her in surprise. "Things were great between us! Don't tell me you weren't satisfied?''

Andrea met his gaze and saw his genuine confusion. She was just as confused until she realized that he was talking about the physical side of their marriage. "The sex was wonderful, Travis. But it wasn't enough. We needed communication, too. You never told me anything about your job as a policeman, how you felt about it…anything about what you did all day.''

"What did you want me say to you? Did you want me to tell you about the abused kids, the battered wives, the crackheads who would kill their mothers for a fix? Maybe you would have liked to hear the story about the fifteen-year-old hooker who stabbed me while I was trying to keep her pimp from bashing her brains out?''

Andrea winced, revolted despite herself.

"Ugly, isn't it? I wanted to protect you from that ugliness and I wanted to protect myself, too."

"You?"

"Yes, me. That little apartment we lived in together was my haven from the war zone I worked in. You were what made it that way. You were calm and beautiful. You made the world seem clean and new to me when I was around you. The last thing I wanted to do was to bring home the ugliness to ruin that. Do you understand?"

"I think I do now, a little. But at the time I felt so alone, so isolated. You didn't confide in me. You didn't share with me. You didn't need me."

"Didn't need you? Your love, the way you gave yourself to me without any questions, without any restraint…that love was all that kept me going, all that kept me sane. Then, suddenly, you turned your back on me just when I needed you the most. I was away, walking a line between life and death, and you left me and filed for divorce."

"You never said you needed me. I thought it was just sex that you needed. Why didn't you tell me how you felt?"

"Why didn't you tell me?"

Andrea had asked herself that question before, and had long ago come to realize that she had unwittingly contributed to the failure of their marriage. "I come from a family of cold people, people who think that discussing one's feelings is in bad taste. I guess we were a pair of emotional cripples, you and I. The only way we ever really communicated was in bed."

Travis smiled ruefully and touched her cheek. "I'm

so sorry, Andi. So sorry for the baby we lost, the surgery, for any pain I caused you. I never meant to hurt you.''

Andrea smiled at his use of her old nickname, and her heart melted when she saw the tears in his eyes. ''I know. I'm sorry, too.''

''Do you still blame me for what happened?'' He asked because he had to know.

Andrea searched her heart for the answer. When she had told Travis about her hysterectomy, she had waited for the illogical surge of shame, the feeling of inadequacy that always accompanied a revelation of her surgery. But this time it hadn't come. It was as if, by finally sharing the truth with him, she'd purged herself of all the old negative emotions she'd been carrying around for years.

''No,'' she whispered. ''It wasn't anyone's fault.''

Their lips came together in a gentle kiss of forgiveness and acceptance and healing. Unexpectedly, it turned into a passionate exploration. Then it became a raging inferno.

Travis slid one big hand up under her shirt. His fingers stroked over the satin cup of her brassiere, turning her nipple into a hard, tight bud. His control stretched as taut as any violin string, he pushed the satin aside and gently rolled the distended, exquisitely sensitive flesh between his thumb and forefinger until Andrea moaned aloud.

Pushing his tongue deeper into her mouth, he eased her back onto the bed. His hand left her breast and moved to the juncture of her thighs, stroking the denim there until it turned hot and damp.

Andrea's hips moved in time to Travis's caresses as she tickled his tongue with her own. She had missed this exquisite insanity, missed loving him. Missed *him*.

She wrapped her legs around him, rubbing against his hardened body, urging him to come to her, to be part of her again.

Travis was on the verge of accepting that invitation when he pulled back and looked down into her face. Her eyes were wide and vulnerable. Full of caring, full of trust. What would they look like after he told her?

What was he doing?

With a groan of pure agony, he pulled away from Andrea and sat up on the foot of the bed. "We have to talk," he said as soon as he could get the words out.

"Now?" Andrea asked in disbelief.

"Yeah, now."

Pulling her clothes into place, Andrea pushed herself up to a sitting position and faced him with foreboding. Somewhere deep in her heart a hope had blossomed. A picture of her and Travis and Bonnie together as a family. She had known it was improbable, unlikely, doomed to failure from the start. But she wished that he had let her cherish it just a little longer.

Travis looked at the floor, not knowing how to begin. There was no right way, no easy way to say what he had to say. He could only make the cut quick and clean, and hope it would hurt less that way. "I'm going away in a few days to kill Tony Valente, the man responsible for my uncle's murder. The man who tracked me down and ordered a hit man to ambush me and Lissa in that mall."

Andrea felt a cold shudder pass through her. She couldn't believe she hadn't put it all together as soon as Travis had told her that the first shooting, in Chicago, had involved organized crime. She'd just been used to thinking of the man who had shot Lissa as some psychopath. She should have known two shootings like that couldn't have been a coincidence. Maybe she hadn't wanted to realize it, hadn't wanted to think that Valente would pursue vengeance so far, for so long.

"That's why you didn't contact the people who helped you last time and arrange to 'die' again!" she said, understanding now. "You were planning to go after Valente all the time. And you don't expect to survive, do you?"

"I'm giving myself the best odds I can. I'm going after them, and they won't expect that. But if I manage to kill Valente, they'll never rest until they track me down."

"And what if, by some miracle, you do survive?"

"*Then* I'll let them give me a new identity, and I'll disappear again."

"Alone?" she asked, already knowing the answer by the expression on his face.

"This time I'm not taking any chances—with Bonnie or with anyone else. If they found me once, they can find me again."

Andrea sat there trying to absorb it all, trying to analyze how she felt. Furious, yes, that was the word. She wanted to argue, to shout, to rage at him until he changed his mind. How could he sit here like this, talking so calmly about going off to die?

She stood up and moved away from the bed. "Nothing will bring your uncle or Lissa back. If you leave Valente alive, you can take Bonnie and disappear with her, and maybe the mob won't be so motivated to find you. But if you kill Valente, you'll stir up a hornet's nest and destroy your chances of getting away!"

Travis got up and came toward her, determined to make her understand. "I shouldn't have run the first time. If I run again, I'll be looking over my shoulder for the rest of my life. I can't live like that."

Andrea felt like shaking him. "You're just disappearing again because it's easier than making a new life, easier than trying to work out your problems and learning to be a father!"

Travis made a gesture of negation. "You're wrong! I want a normal life with normal problems more than I've ever wanted anything. But I lost Lissa because I thought I could beat the mob. I'm not going to risk another innocent life by trying it a second time."

Frustrated, angry, wounded, Andrea backed out of the room, away from him. "Nothing's really changed in five years!"

Travis looked at her, craving her understanding and not getting it. "It sure hasn't," he agreed bitterly, slamming the door shut behind her.

Andrea ran into her own room and threw herself down on her bed. She lay there staring at the darkened ceiling unseeingly, wishing it were all some kind of bad dream or practical joke. But she knew this nightmare was all too real. When Travis disappeared this time, it would be forever.

Chapter Eight

Andrea lay on her bed and watched the room grow lighter by degrees.

She'd tossed and turned all night trying to think through the anger and the hurt. But there was only one conclusion she could come to, only one course left open to her. Acceptance.

Despite her best efforts, she had failed to convince Travis to change his mind. And if he was determined to go on his suicide mission, then she wanted Bonnie.

She got up and walked the short distance to Travis's room. The door was open, and Travis was inside throwing clothing into an open suitcase on the bed.

Andrea rubbed her arms as a sudden chill went through her. Travis talking about leaving and the sight of him actually packing to go were two different things. She was losing him for the second time, and there was nothing she could do to prevent it.

Travis looked up and saw her framed in his doorway, dressed in that pristine, yet oh-so-provocative white nightgown. Sunlight, streaming in through the window behind her, made the cotton all but transparent.

Travis felt a wave of longing so sharp that it was actually painful, not just for sex, or even for Andrea, but for what she represented. He was going off to die, and she was standing there tempting him to stay and live. She was the perfect lure, a combination of sensual woman and sunlight-wrapped angel. It was a picture he would carry in his mind and his heart for every minute of the time that was left to him.

He finally managed to wrest his gaze away. "Come to say goodbye?" he asked, torn between wishing she hadn't come to torment him and gratitude that she had.

"I've come to talk to you about Bonnie."

He looked up at her then. She stepped out of the sunlight and into the room, becoming just an ordinary woman again. A woman with tangled hair and worried eyes. A woman he needed to take into his arms as much as he needed the air he breathed.

Instead, he walked back to the closet and took another shirt off a hanger. "I've been thinking about Bonnie, too. I understand now why having her means so much to you."

He paused, struggling to find the words. He only had one thing left to give her and he wanted to do it right. "I'd be grateful if you'd take care of her for me. There's no time for a formal adoption, and I won't be around to testify to my intentions. So I... Would you like to marry me before I leave? There's a waiting period, but anyone can get that waived with a judge's signature. As my wife, no one would challenge your right to adopt Bonnie. And after Travis Hunter 'disappears,' you can divorce me for desertion.''

Stunned by his proposition, Andrea stared at him. She wanted Bonnie, yes. And she loved Travis. But to participate in some farce of a marriage…

He folded the shirt and laid it in the suitcase. ''My flight to Chicago is taking off from San Antonio tonight. If you drive there with me, we can get married before I leave.''

Was it to be like this, then? So cold, so unfeeling, like some clandestine business deal? She remembered him saying that love didn't exist for him anymore. Now she finally believed it. But love or no love, she still wanted Bonnie. And he had been right about one thing. So many things could go wrong with an adoption.

She had a feeling that there was so much she ought to say, yet only two words came to her. ''All right.''

The ensuing silence was broken by Bonnie's demand for her morning bottle, and Andrea left the room without expressing any of the conflicting emotions raging in her heart.

''I would say congratulations, Travis, but, somehow, that just doesn't seem appropriate.''

Jude seemed to have spoken for all of them.

Rob, Jenny, Jude and Maggie had spent the last hour gathered around the dining room table at Landon Ranch. They had worn identical expressions of disbelief and bewilderment as Travis and Andrea had tried to explain Travis's past as Trey Morgan, his up-coming trip to Chicago and their decision to marry.

Now Travis looked at each of the Emorys in turn. "I just want you to understand," he told them. "It's not that I didn't love Lissa. And I don't mean any disrespect to her memory by remarrying so soon. But—"

Jenny reached across the table and took his hand, bringing his flow of words to a halt. "I think all of us have been hoping that you and Andrea would get back together—for Bonnie's sake as well as your own. We understand, and I know Lissa would, too. What I think we're having a problem with is this…this mission you're going on."

"Isn't there any way to get at this Valente character legally?" Rob wanted to know.

"No way that anyone has been able to find so far," Travis said. "I'm not going to waste time trying to come up with some other way of getting to him while he sends another hit man after me. And I'm not going to run and hide. If he found me once, he can do it again."

No one spoke for a moment as they all absorbed the finality of what he was saying.

Jude shifted in his chair and ran a hand over his jaw. "I wish there was some way for us to back you up, but this is way out of our league."

"You *can* back me up," Travis responded. "By wishing me luck."

Jude gave him a cynical smile. "You're sure as hell gonna need it, *amigo*."

Maggie looked at Andrea. "Are you and Bonnie flying back to Chicago with Travis?"

Andrea thought about it, pictured herself alone with the baby in her lakeside condominium, waiting for the news bulletin that would tell her a body had been found; wondering if the report was true or if Travis had simply disappeared again.

"I'd like to stay on at the ranch for a while, if that's all right with all of you."

"Of course it's all right," Jenny assured her. "You need your friends around you at a time like this."

The words gave Andrea a warm feeling in spite of her apprehension about the future.

"If you had known about all of this ahead of time," Jenny continued, "we could have gone to San Antonio with you for the ceremony. But there are so many activities scheduled for today, and I have five calls to go out on."

Maggie chimed in, "But at least I can watch Bonnie for you while you're gone."

Andrea, who had been dreading the thought of subjecting the baby to the long car trip, readily agreed. "Thank you. That will be a big help. I'll be back just as soon as I can."

"Don't be silly! It's your wedding day. Relax, eat out in a restaurant—spend the night. Bonnie will be fine."

Andrea felt like a fraud. She was marrying a man who didn't love her, who would be leaving her in only a few hours. Just the idea of a romantic wedding night was all but unbearable. But she didn't want to spoil the illusion for the others, so she smiled a gracious acceptance.

Rob had stowed Andrea's overnight bag and Travis's suitcase in the trunk of her rental car, and everything was ready to go.

Andrea ducked back into the hallway and made her way to the nursery, wanting a moment alone with Bonnie before she left. But when she reached her destination, she saw that someone else had had the same idea.

Travis stood there holding his daughter and singing her a lullaby. It sounded a little off-key to Andrea, and some of the words were wrong, but Bonnie seemed fascinated by the big, blue-eyed crooner. She lay utterly still, peering up at him intently, one small hand clutching at his bearded cheek.

Tears came to Andrea's eyes, and she had to bite her lip to keep a sob from escaping.

The song ended, and Travis looked up and saw her. He gave her a self-conscious smile. "I was just, uh…"

Andrea stepped forward and touched Bonnie's silky soft hand, so tiny against her own. "I came to say goodbye, too."

But she would be back soon. Travis wouldn't be coming back at all. Her heart raged at the unfairness of it. But there was nothing she could do.

"Listen, would you do something for me?" he said.

Andrea looked up at him.

"When she gets older and starts asking questions

about me, would you...would you make sure she knows that her father loved her?''

"Yes," Andrea said, when she could trust her voice again. "I'll make sure she knows."

The rest of the day held a strange sense of déjà vu for Andrea. The long car drive, answering the necessary questions to get the marriage license. Even the ceremony in the judge's chambers. Of course, it had been a justice of the peace who had married them the first time, but the words were almost the same. The ring was a plain gold band like the one she'd been given seven years ago. The vows hadn't changed. And for Andrea, at least, the feelings were the same. She only wished that this time the outcome could be different. That this time, the bride and groom would get a chance to live happily ever after.

"...I now pronounce you man and wife."

Travis's lips came down on hers with such sweet possessiveness that she half believed a happy ending was possible. But wasn't every bride entitled to a few illusions on her wedding day?

Andrea's shattered with an almost audible crack mere seconds after they left the judge's chambers.

"Listen, Andrea, I'm sorry I gave you such a hard time over the last two weeks. I know you'll be a good mother to Bonnie. Take care of yourself."

He had begun to walk away from her before she could even absorb the fact that he was saying goodbye.

She plunged after him, trying her best to keep up with his long-legged stride. "Wait! Don't you need a ride to the airport?"

"I'll take a cab."

"But your plane doesn't leave until tonight."

"I'll have lunch at the airport, buy a book to read."

He came to a halt at the elevator, and she almost ran into his back.

"Couldn't we have lunch together?" she suggested a little desperately as the chime sounded and the doors slid open.

They boarded the empty car, and he looked at her for the first time since they'd exchanged vows. "Ah, hell, Andi! The longer we stretch this out, the more it's going to hurt. The last thing you want is a long drawn-out goodbye."

Andrea knew he was right. It was better to end it here, like this. That was the safe, sensible thing to do. But it wasn't what she wanted.

Suddenly, it came to her. She was still doing what she'd done throughout their first marriage—hiding her feelings because she was afraid to admit she really needed another human being, afraid of being hurt. She hadn't gotten remarried just for Bonnie. She wanted Travis. She wanted whatever happiness she could steal before he left. And she didn't care what price she had to pay in pain.

She threw her arms around his neck and smiled up at him. "I think a long drawn-out goodbye is *exactly* what I want!"

Then she gave him a kiss that left no doubt at all as to what she meant.

When they finally drew apart, they were both shaking, and he looked like a man who had been offered a gift he wanted above everything, but didn't dare take. "Are you sure, Andi? It's not going to change my mind about leaving—nothing is going to do that. I don't want to hurt you."

She touched his face and smiled. "I'm going to hurt, anyway, so I might as well grab whatever happiness I can. I could use a few more happy memories of Travis Hunter."

"And I'm sure going to enjoy giving them to you." With a grin of pure anticipation, he pulled her into his arms and kissed her again.

They checked into the most expensive hotel in town and, while he soaked in the huge Roman tub, she ordered champagne, steak, lobster and a dozen other items from room service.

When the food arrived, Andrea started to call Travis out of the bathroom, then another idea occurred to her.

During their marriage, he had been the one to seduce her, to draw her out, to make her forget her inhibitions. *He* had always been the one to make love to *her*. Now she wanted to be the one to reach out to him, to give him pleasure. If all they had left was just these few hours together, she wanted to make that time into a memory that he would carry with him forever.

The soft tapping on the bathroom door roused Travis from a state of near slumber. Andrea. The food must have arrived. Smiling in anticipation of more than just the meal, he gathered himself to get out of the huge tub.

"Travis, would you mind if I brought the food in there?"

He sank down into a swirl of hot water, surprised and a little intrigued by her request. All kinds of interesting possibilities suggested themselves to him, and the smile became a grin. "Sure. Why not?"

He watched as the door swung slowly open. She entered, carrying a heavily laden tray. Her makeup and hair were as perfect as always, but he couldn't figure out what she was wearing. Above the tray, her arms and upper chest were exposed. Below, he saw bare feet and a pair of long, luscious legs he had been dreaming about for years. They ended in a triangle of peach colored silk that looked more like a decoration than an article of clothing.

Andrea came to a halt, sinking to her knees in front of him with a grace that any geisha would have envied. Then she set the tray down beside her on the tile floor.

If Travis had been slumped down a little lower in the tub, he might have drowned. He stared at her, mesmerized by the unexpected sight of her bare breasts. Andrea, who had always wanted to get dressed and undressed in privacy, who had felt self-conscious if they didn't make love in the dark—that Andrea was serving him lunch *topless*.

The shock of it seemed to go straight to his groin and carry the punch of an electric current. Whatever lethargy his long soak in the hot water had induced vanished instantly, and he sat up straight, on the verge of leaping out of the tub and grabbing her. He never got the chance.

Smiling down at him angelically, as if nothing was even the least bit out of the ordinary, Andrea leaned forward and used her fingers to pop a bit of buttered lobster into his half-open mouth. "Do you like it?" she asked.

Travis managed to catch the edge of one finger with his tongue before she withdrew it, but he was fantasizing about softer, pinker parts of her anatomy. He felt another hard tug in a very sensitive area and wanted to groan aloud. If she couldn't see just how much he liked it, then she must be blind! "They're beautiful," he managed to choke out. "I mean, it's fine."

"I was surprised at you today," Andrea said, secretly reveling in the effect she was having on him. What she hadn't quite anticipated was the hot excitement that was building in her own body in response to his obvious arousal.

She took a bit of lobster for herself, then carefully wiped her hands on a large linen napkin, willing herself to concentrate on what she was saying instead of the way her husband was looking at her. "I didn't think you would call all the Emorys together and explain everything. Somehow I thought you'd tell them you were going back to San Antonio, then just disappear."

"I was planning to," Travis said, eyeing the twin temptations that dangled just out of reach as he took another morsel of food from her hands. He ached to reach out and caress her, but he was afraid it would be a violation of the rules in this delicious game she was playing. "It would have been a lot simpler and a lot safer to leave without an explanation. But, in the end, I just couldn't do it. I think they're the only real friends I've ever had."

Andrea looked at him in surprise. "Me, too." She smiled. "Do you think we're actually becoming compatible?"

He gave her a wicked grin. "Oh, we were always compatible, Andi. In some areas."

She fed him a piece of steak and licked her own lips, enjoying this new kind of foreplay. "Are the Emorys really the only friends you've ever had?" she asked, finding it hard to believe that he had been just as isolated as she had. "What about when you were with the department? You had plenty of friends."

"Acquaintances. I never let anyone get close enough to me to be my friend, except maybe…"

He paused and a shadow crossed his face. For just a moment, he forgot the sensuous teasing match they were involved in and let unpleasant memories crowd in on him.

"Who?" Andrea prompted, hating the fact that her time with him had been invaded by the ugliness of reality, but needing to know.

"Tony Valente."

Andrea stared at him. "You mean, the man you're going to…? *That* Tony Valente?"

"The longer I was undercover, the more my identity as a cop began to blur. There were times…there were times when I *was* the man I was pretending to be. One day, there was an attempt on Tony's life, and I stepped in and saved him. Me, the guy who wanted to see him dead."

He shook his head as if he still couldn't understand how it had happened. "After that, Tony made me one of his bodyguards, and he considered me a friend. I began to think of him as almost...admirable. A man of honor known for keeping his word. I had to keep reminding myself how he made his money, how many people were hurt by what his organization did.''

''And given all that, you don't have any regrets about...about what you plan to do?''

Travis's eyes seemed to darken and his voice grew cold. ''After what happened in the mall, I have no regrets whatsoever about killing Valente. I only regret that I have to leave you and Bonnie behind in order to do it.''

You and Bonnie. It wasn't exactly a declaration of love, but it was enough for Andrea. She knew she couldn't change his mind, and she had given reality enough of the precious moments remaining to them. It was time to return to the fantasy. A fantasy in which she and her husband were the only two people in existence, and tomorrow was a concept that had no meaning.

Reaching toward the tray, she retrieved the already-opened bottle of champagne from its ice bucket. She took a delicate sip straight from the bottle, deliberately allowing some of the ice-cold fluid to dribble down her chin and onto her chest. She drew in her breath sharply as it reached one nipple, causing the hardened flesh to draw even tighter.

''Oops!'' she said, feeling a little foolish as she ran one finger down her breast to catch the tiny trickle of fine wine. She brought the digit to her mouth and licked it clean, smiling up at Travis from beneath lowered lashes.

Travis forgot all about the past and the rules of the

game. He launched himself out of the water, looking as intimidating and savage as some ancient sea god. Throwing himself on top of his wife, he pressed her down against the tile, scattering the remains of their feast and overturning the champagne bottle.

Andrea didn't notice. Now her world consisted only of Travis. She felt the shock of his burning hot body as it covered her cool one. Heard the satisfied sounds he made as he devoured her breasts, licking them, suckling them until her body burned just as hot as his.

She buried her fingers in his dark hair, trying to pull him closer, longing to become a part of him. But he only moved farther down along the quivering skin of her belly, lowering her panties inch by inch.

Andrea suddenly tensed, realizing what he intended. ''Wait,'' she whispered. ''I was planning on getting into the tub with you.''

Travis looked up at her, feeling her hesitation and trying to divine the cause of it. Then it dawned on him what she was so concerned about.

''There isn't anything about the scent or taste of soap and water that turns me on, Andi. I want you exactly the way you are.''

With a soft sigh of appreciation, he lowered his head and pressed his lips against the most sensitive part of her body.

Feeling the hot, wet caress of his tongue inside and out, Andrea moaned his name and arched her back against the cool tile. Then she felt his hands slide up over her rib cage to cover her breasts. He kneaded the tender flesh gently, lightly squeezing her sensitive nipples between his fingers.

Andrea cried out as her body shattered into a billion shimmering pieces, and Travis continued to stroke her, taking her from one climax to the next with scarcely a heartbeat in between.

Then he was above her, inside her, making her fight for every breath again as his hard thrusts built on the remnants of the pleasure he had already given her, extending it, heightening it, taking her over the edge once more.

Arms and legs wrapped around Travis, Andrea clung to him, whimpering in response to each movement of his body. He lowered his head and gave her a deep, slow kiss that seemed to mesh their souls, bonding them together as if they had never been apart.

He held the kiss as he came, gasping against her lips, writhing in her arms, his body seeking and somehow finding an even deeper haven inside her.

Finally, they lay still, exhausted, covered with a fine sheen of perspiration, until they were able to breathe easily once more. Then Travis raised his head and tried to pull away, but Andrea held him securely.

"Let me get up, sweetheart. I must be crushing you."

"You are, but it feels good."

Travis rolled them both over on their sides. "Better?"

"Umm," Andrea said softly, knowing she couldn't possibly feel any better no matter what he did. She didn't want to spoil that feeling, but she couldn't resist voicing the question that was burning in her mind.

"Was it any different?" she asked, tentatively.

Travis pulled back to look at her face. "Different than what?"

"Different than it was before my...my operation."

Travis couldn't quite stop himself from chuckling. After what they had just shared, how could she still find reason to doubt herself? "Hell, yes," he told her. "It was different. It was better!"

Andrea closed her eyes and recited a silent prayer of thanks. When she opened them again, the first thing she noticed was his scar. She had seen it earlier, of course, but she had forced herself to ignore it. It had been too threatening, too intrusive to be part of the fantasy that had sustained her all day. But she couldn't ignore it any longer.

It wasn't like his old scar, white and faded with time. It was new, and red and angry, running down from his shoulder and nearly halfway across his chest. A banner that told at a glance how badly he'd been hurt, how close he'd come to dying. And now he was going into danger again.

Suddenly, despite her resolve, Andrea was crying in Travis's arms, crying and telling him how much she loved him.

Ignoring the pain in his shoulder, Travis picked her up and carried her to the bed. Then he lay down beside her and held her, smoothing her hair, wiping away her tears, and feeling helpless and overwhelmed. Andrea had never cried in front of him before, had never left herself that open, that vulnerable. Now it seemed her tears would never end.

Why had he been so weak? Why had he made love to her when he'd known it would only hurt her in the end? And what could he do to help her now? He wanted to stay, to delay their parting. But the only way he could keep her safe was to leave. And if he didn't go soon, he knew he never would.

Knowing of no other way to comfort her, Travis made love to her again, as slowly and sweetly and gently as he could. He held her against his heart until she fell asleep in his arms. Then, forcing himself away from her, he dressed and slipped out of the room.

When Andrea awoke, it was dark, and she knew from the hollow feeling inside her that he was gone and she was alone. The pain came sharp and fresh, as if a part of her had been slashed away. But she could summon no regrets. Because for one shining moment, she'd had it all.

Chapter Nine

"It's about time you got here!"

Mike Manelli stepped back and allowed Travis to enter the high-rise apartment, then closed the door behind him.

Travis spared a quick glance at the spectacular moonlit view of Lake Michigan. Then he quickly averted his gaze. There were too many memories. Memories of his life here as Trey Morgan. His life with Andrea. A life that was over. Just like his life as Travis Hunter was over now. The pain that thought brought with it almost took his breath away.

Ruthlessly blocking all thoughts of his wife from his mind, he turned toward his employee. "Talk to me."

Mike made a face. "As usual. Mr. Personality." He settled himself comfortably on the large sofa, spread his arms out across the backrest and looked up at Travis.

"Well, as you know, I've been following Mr. Valente around for two weeks now. And the time he's most vulnerable, the best time to get to him, is on one of his visits to his mistress's apartment. Which happens to be in this building."

"It's nice to know I'm not just paying for the view," Travis said dryly. He walked to the bar, opened the small refrigerator and popped the top on a can of beer as Mike continued his report.

"I rented this apartment under an assumed name. It's directly above the girlfriend's. Being a good neighbor, I helped her carry some packages up a few days ago, and she asked me in for a drink. I got an impression of her key—which I used to make a copy—the code to her security system and her phone number."

"Phone number?" Travis echoed quizzically.

"I figure that you get in place outside the front door, then I dial her number. Her living room phone rings, and Valente's bodyguard goes to answer it. That takes him out of sight of the front door, and that's when you let yourself in. I'll pretend to have a wrong number or something, try to keep him talking as long as I can."

"No answering machine? No extension in the bedroom?"

"No answering machine. And the lady unplugs the phone in the bedroom when she's, uh, entertaining."

Travis lifted an eyebrow. "I thought you said she asked you in for a *drink?*"

"While she was mixing it, I excused myself to use the bathroom and planted a bug in her bedroom. I've got her last session with Valente on tape, if you care to listen.''

''Anything significant?''

''Just the fact that she unplugs the phone. And that Valente's coming back around eleven tonight.''

''Good,'' Travis said, relieved that it would be so soon. Every minute he had to wait was an agony, another temptation to change his mind. ''Start packing up your belongings. As soon as you get off the phone with that bodyguard, clear out of here. Leave the car you rented parked outside for me to use, take a cab to the airport, fly back to San Antonio and forget you were ever here.''

Mike leaned forward. ''You don't want me to come in and back you up?''

Travis finished his beer and set the empty can back on the bar. ''Why, so we can trip over each other? This only takes one man.''

''And one gun, right? I've been asking myself what the hell this is all about, and there's only one answer I can come up with. You don't bust in to see the head of the most powerful Mafia family in Chicago just to chat. You're going to blow him away, aren't you? Because somehow, some way, he's responsible for Lissa's death.''

Travis kept his face expressionless, knowing that he would only be endangering Mike's life if he revealed any more. ''I don't pay you to ask questions. I pay you to follow orders.''

Manelli leapt up off the couch and moved across the room to face him. ''I thought we were friends!''

''You thought wrong.'' He started to move away,

but a hand on his arm halted his progress. He turned his head and met Mike's concerned gaze.

"If you live after you do this thing, Travis, they won't stop looking until they find you. Have you thought about that?"

"Yes, I have." Travis shrugged away from the other man's grasp and his concern, conveying without words that the subject was closed. "Now let's go over the floor plan."

Travis got off the elevator and surveyed the empty hallway. So far, so good. Moving quickly, he covered the distance to his goal. Pausing in front of the apartment belonging to Valente's mistress, he put his ear close to the door.

He heard the sound of a television, but no phone ringing. Muscles tensed, he counted off one minute, then two. What in the hell was Mike waiting for?

He willed himself to relax, knowing that impatience could be deadly in his line of work. People who rushed things made stupid mistakes and ended up dead. But maybe he wouldn't mind that so much if it put an end to the agony he'd been feeling since he'd left Andrea.

He couldn't forget how she'd cried in his arms, and he cursed himself again for not leaving her in the hallway outside the judge's chambers as he'd originally planned. He remembered the last thing she'd said to him just before she'd finally drifted off to sleep: "Promise. Promise that if you survive, you'll send me a sign. Something so that I'll know you're alive... somewhere."

He had promised. He'd told her that, if he lived,

he'd send her a single red rose, no address, no card. Now he smiled cynically at the memory. Where he'd gotten that pretty notion, he couldn't say. Some latent streak of romanticism, he guessed. Of course, he would never send it. He wouldn't be cruel enough to leave her worrying and wondering about him for the rest of her days. Let her think it had ended here. Let the freedom to build a new life be the last gift he gave to her.

The sound of a ringing phone broke into his thoughts and sent a surge of adrenaline through his system. It rang once, twice, three times. And then it stopped.

Travis inserted the copy of the key into the lock, turned it and pushed open the door. But after giving only a few inches, it refused to move any farther. Travis looked up and saw that the chain lock was engaged. Grateful for Mike's careful preparation, he removed a bolt cutter from a special pocket inside his jacket and used it to cut the chain.

Returning the tool to his pocket, he opened the door and eased inside. Then he grasped the doorknob in one gloved hand and quietly closed the door behind him. Quickly, he entered the code he'd memorized into the security system and deactivated it.

Moving forward into the dimly lit foyer, sneakered feet sinking deeply into the plush carpet, he pulled a plastic bag from his pants pocket. He inched into the hallway and passed the darkened kitchen. He could hear the dialogue from the living room TV clearly now, but no phone conversation. He could see the big sofa, a coffee table, the sliding glass doors that led to the balcony. No bodyguard.

Travis approached the entrance to the living room, mentally reviewing the apartment's floor plan and furniture arrangement. To return from where the phone was located to a seat that would give him a view of the television, the guard would have to pass by him. All he had to do was wait.

Then, abruptly, the unexpected happened. The bodyguard turned into the hallway that led to the kitchen, the front door, and Travis. The other man's eyes widened, and his hand moved toward the gun in his shoulder holster. His mouth opened, but, before any sound could emerge, a blow from Travis temporarily paralyzed his larynx.

They went down together, the sound of their fall deadened by the thick carpet. The man managed to strike a glancing blow to Travis's wounded shoulder and draw his gun halfway out the holster before Travis could pull the chloroform-soaked cloth from the plastic bag he carried. He pressed the cloth over the man's nose and mouth and used all the strength he had to hold it in place the few seconds it took for the man to lose consciousness. Then he returned the cloth to the bag, sealed it and pocketed it.

He staggered to his feet, trying to breathe through the pain. Drawing an unregistered gun that he'd picked up during his police days, he screwed on the silencer and moved to the closed door of the bedroom.

He heard the sound of the shower running and hoped that it was the mistress who was in the bathroom—and that she was alone. It would be a lot less complicated that way.

Travis took a deep breath, trying to focus his thoughts. An image of Andrea filled his mind, and mentally he said his final goodbye.

Then he kicked open the door and rushed into the bedroom.

Valente was in the bed alone. Even as Travis registered that fact, he saw Valente pull a gun out from under a pillow and level it at him. At the same instant, Travis got Valente squarely in his sights.

Travis was willing to die with Valente—he was under a death sentence by Valente's order, anyway, so he had nothing to lose. But as his finger tightened on the trigger, Valente spoke.

"Hold it a minute! We can talk this over, make a deal."

Despite his resolve, Travis hesitated. The sound of Valente's voice brought memories rushing back. Memories of a friendship Travis wanted no part of.

"Goodbye is the only thing we have left to say to each other, Tony."

Travis saw what looked like bewilderment, then a sudden flash of recognition in Valente's dark gaze. "Son of a gun! I'd know those blue eyes and that bad attitude anywhere. You always did have more guts than brains." A sardonic smile curved Valente's mouth. "You're looking very good for a man who's been dead for five years, Trey. Or maybe I should call you Johnny Angelo for old times' sake? Of course, you probably have a brand-new name by now."

Travis felt his hand begin to tremble and willed

himself to hold it steady. "Don't pretend you don't know exactly what's going on, Tony. That won't save you. Nothing will. I'm here to do what I should have done years ago. I'm going to kill you for ordering the hit on my uncle."

The last response he had expected was the sound of Valente's laughter. "I don't order hits on cops. It's very bad for my business." He eyed Travis appraisingly. "You wearing a wire again, Trey?"

Slowly, never taking his eyes or the gun off Valente, Travis used his left hand to pull his shirt up and expose his chest. "I don't need a wire this time, Tony, because you're never going to live to see the inside of a courtroom."

"I hate to disappoint you, but I didn't order your uncle's death. Maury Romano—you remember him, Trey? The dummy you taped bragging about how he shot your uncle? Well, he did the job on his own. Your uncle interrupted Maury when he was in the middle of conducting a little business—"

"You mean while he was committing cold-blooded murder."

Valente shrugged. "I won't quibble over the words. The result of this interruption was that, instead of laying down a little cover fire and getting the hell out of there, Maury panicked and wasted your uncle. And after Maury was sentenced to prison, he also arranged to have you shot down in that alley in revenge for testifying against him."

Travis thought it over, and the first flicker of doubt stirred to life inside him. He squelched it ruthlessly.

"And I'm supposed to believe that you're totally innocent?" he said, his voice heavy with cynicism.

As if he could sense his adversary wavering, Valente pressed his case. "I don't remember a time when I was ever totally innocent. For instance, Maury Romano was knifed to death in prison."

"You're saying you had your own man killed?"

"He was warned, and he chose not to listen. He became too much of a liability to me. So it seems that I took care of your revenge for you. As far as I can see, we have no argument between us."

"There's the little matter of my late wife," Travis said, grateful that the familiar, righteous anger was finally rising up to claim him.

Valente frowned, his eyes narrowing. "Your wife?"

Enraged at the pretense of ignorance, Travis almost spat out the words. "A gunman came after me in a Texas mall a little over a month ago. He wounded me, and he killed my wife. If everyone in your organization thinks I'm dead, then who sent that man after me?"

"I have no idea," Valente told him evenly.

Travis's finger compressed the trigger another fraction of a millimeter. "You're lying!"

"I may be a lot of things, but I'm no liar. You should remember that, Trey. As far as I knew, Trey Morgan died five years ago. I'm willing to leave it at that. Are you?"

It was just a lie, a denial that Valente was using in an attempt to save his own life. But what if it was the truth? "You want to call things even between us,

Tony? I didn't think you were one to forgive a betrayal of trust so easily.''

"I'm not. I remember that you betrayed me, truly betrayed me. You weren't just another stupid cop doing his job. You became my friend, almost my brother, and then you tried to destroy me.''

Valente looked at Travis, his anger obvious. But his control of that emotion was just as obvious. ''At first, I did want revenge. But I thought it over. I remembered that you once saved my life when you could have let me die. Because of that and because of the unfortunate incident with your uncle, I was—and I am—willing to be generous.''

Seeing the truth in Valente's eyes, Travis slowly lowered his gun.

A heartbeat later, Valente did the same.

They held each other's gaze for a moment longer before Travis deliberately turned his back and walked toward the doorway.

''Trey…''

Travis turned back to face the other man, half expecting to be met by a bullet. But all Valente gave him was a smile that chilled his blood. ''Don't ever come after me again, Trey. This time, you had the angels on your side. Next time, you won't live to walk away.''

Travis walked out the front door of the apartment building feeling shaky, light-headed, and a little disoriented, like a condemned prisoner who had received a last-minute pardon.

He was stunned by the outcome of his confrontation

with Valente. For the first time in five years, the sword hanging over his head was gone. He could go wherever he wanted to go, do whatever he wanted to. Which meant he could go back to Andrea and Bonnie. But, no, he couldn't do that until he was sure they'd be safe in his company. Until he found out the identity of the gunman in the mall.

Who else would want Travis Hunter dead? He couldn't think of anyone. Maybe the gunman *had* been a psychopath, choosing victims at random. But if that were the case, why hadn't the man just kept on shooting as he moved through the crowd? Why had he and Lissa been the only ones attacked?

Again, he had the tantalizing feeling that he was missing something, but, try as he might, he just couldn't pinpoint what it was.

As Travis approached the rental car, the shadowy form behind the steering wheel sent his hand to his gun again before he realized it was Mike. With a sigh of relief, he climbed into the passenger seat, and Manelli sped away in the direction of the airport.

Travis gave himself a few minutes to savor the beauty of the night and the new chance at life he'd been given before he spoke. ''I thought I told you not to get involved in this, Mike.''

''I don't call this getting involved. If you hadn't come out of there in ten more minutes, I was going in after you. *That* would have been getting involved.''

''You are one crazy hombre, Michael,'' Travis said, the tone of his words turning criticism into compliment.

Mike gave him a cocky smile. ''So I've been told,

but I have nothing on you.'' Then his smile faded, and his expression turned serious. ''You're way too mellow for someone who just wasted a man of Valente's persuasion, my friend. Just what the hell did happen back there?''

After a second of hesitation, Travis reached a decision. He glanced at his watch and saw that it was after one in the morning. ''Buy me a sandwich and coffee, and I'll tell you a bedtime story.''

''Sure, why not?'' Mike agreed with a stifled yawn. ''I have an expense account.''

At the airport, they found that the first available flight to San Antonio didn't leave until around ten a.m. They purchased their tickets, then walked to the airport coffee shop.

An hour later, they'd finished their snack and Travis had finished explaining about his former life as Trey Morgan, as well as relating what had happened in the apartment with Valente.

Mike could only shake his head in disbelief. ''I had some wild theories, but they didn't even come close! Now I see why that Andrea Ballanger was so determined to find you.''

Travis couldn't stop the smile that curled his lips at the mention of her name. ''She's Andrea Hunter now.''

Mike rubbed at his forehead. ''You mean you married her? Again?''

Travis launched into another round of explanations that lasted for the time it took to drink one more cup of coffee.

''I'm looking forward to getting back to my family,'' he concluded. ''There's just one thing stopping me.''

''If Valente wasn't responsible for the attack on you in the mall, then who was?'' Mike thought about it. ''What about someone from your days as a cop? Maybe someone you helped put away happened to recognize you as Trey Morgan and decided to get even.''

Travis tapped his fingers against the tabletop. ''I can't remember anyone who would want to kill me— beat me up or break my legs maybe, but not blow me away. Besides, I didn't recognize that guy in the mall. I'm sure I never saw him before that day.''

''What about that Jack Keel guy? The one you were supposed to be working for when you met Lissa. He could have hired someone to do you in.''

''I don't think he ever found out I was being paid to spy on him. And, even if he did, I doubt he'd consider it a strong enough motive for murder.''

''Still, it's somewhere to start. I'll get on it as soon as we get back to the office.''

They left the coffee shop and settled down in adjacent chairs to doze away the hours remaining until their flight.

Travis, worn-out from his earlier exertions and still recuperating from his wounds, expected to sleep soundly. Instead, he once again dreamed of Lissa's killing.

It all replayed itself in his mind. The mall, the crowd. Lissa's hand on his arm, the fear in her eyes. The stranger pulling a gun.

He felt the impact of the bullets, the helplessness, the guilt, the grief. The terrible finality of his loss.

And then it began all over again....

Travis awoke with a start to find his face wet with tears. Swiping at his eyes, he looked around to see if anyone had noticed, but Mike was still sleeping soundly in the chair next to his.

After checking his watch, he shook Manelli awake. "Come on, it's getting late. We don't want to miss our plane."

Standing up, he ran a hand through his hair and stretched, careful of his protesting shoulder. He was about to start for the departure gate, when he saw a sign advertising roses for sale.

With Mike trailing behind him and complaining all the way, Travis purchased a single red rose at the gift shop.

They had to stand in line to pay for it, and Mike glanced at his watch with a grimace. "I bet you're not even gonna tell me what's so important about that damned flower, are you?"

"No way in hell," Travis assured him.

They were just stepping out of the shop, when Mike grabbed his arm. Travis whipped around to see a look of alarm in the other man's eyes. He was reaching for his weapon when Mike laughed and shook his head.

"Sorry, Travis," he said a little sheepishly. "I saw a man who looked like one of Valente's men coming toward us. I spend two weeks shadowing the mob, and I turn into a basket case!"

Suddenly, the airport sights and sounds seemed to fade out for Travis and, once again, he was back in the shopping mall. He saw the fear in Lissa's eyes as the stranger walked toward them, felt the way her hand tightened on his arm. And the man hadn't drawn his gun yet, hadn't done anything threatening.

At last, Travis knew what had been bothering him for so long. Lissa had recognized her killer, had known that he meant to harm her! Travis had been so sure that it was his fault, so sure a hit man sent by Valente had done the job, that he hadn't even stopped to consider the possibility that Lissa had been the man's main target.

And the only one he knew who would ever want to hurt Lissa was that no-good ex-husband of hers, Ted Shafer.

"What is it? What's wrong?"

Travis looked into Mike's concerned face, then brushed past him. "There's no time now. I'll explain later."

"You're damned right there's no time! We're about to miss our... Hey, where are you going now?"

Travis walked to a nearby pay phone, dropped a quarter into the slot and entered his calling-card number. It rang through. "Let me talk to Dan Gonzalez, please. Tell him it's Travis Hunter and that it's an emergency."

"You're calling our police contact in San Antonio? Why? We'll be there in a couple of hours—if you hurry up!"

Travis held a finger to his lips, signaling Mike to silence as Gonzalez came on the line. "I'm about to catch a flight out of Chicago, Dan, and I need some information before I leave. I think Lissa's ex-husband, Ted Shafer, may have been the gunman in the mall. I'd like you to call the warden at Huntsville Prison for me and find out if Shafer was released and when. If he was, I need to find him before he decides to come after me or my daughter again. Let me give you my number here.''

Travis hung up, took a deep breath, and turned to answer Mike's questions. He had just finished when the pay phone rang.

He grabbed the receiver. ''Talk to me.''

''You may be right about all this, Travis,'' Gonzalez told him. ''The warden said that Shafer got out of prison the week before the mall shooting. He never showed up for his first meeting with his parole officer, and no one knows where he is now. His last known address was his mom's home in Austin. Here's her number….''

Travis fumbled in his jacket pocket for a pen and jotted down the number on the tattered cover of a phone book. ''Thanks, Dan. I really owe you one. Leave a message for me at the agency if you find out anything else.''

''You were right, weren't you?'' Mike said. ''Shafer's out.''

Travis tried to subdue the feeling of imminent danger that had him by the throat, but it refused to go away. ''Promise them anything,'' he told Mike as he started to dial again. ''But get them to hold that damned plane!''

He watched Mike jog away, then his attention was pulled back to the phone as a feminine voice answered. ''Mrs. Shafer?''

''Yes. Who is this?''

He didn't waste words. ''My name is Travis Hunter.

I married your former daughter-in-law, Lissa, after she divorced Ted. Lissa was shot and killed in San Antonio a month and a half ago, and I have reason to believe that your son did it. I think he may come after me or my daughter again, and I want you to help me. I want you to tell me where he is.''

There was a long pause, followed by a horrified cry. "Lissa's dead? Oh, no!''

Travis forced himself to cut off her tearful questions. "Do you know where he is?''

"Ted did stay with me for a while after he got out of prison, but I haven't seen him for about six weeks. He left one morning and just never came back.''

That information fit right in with Travis's expectations. Shafer had disappeared around the day of the shooting. "Do you have any idea where he might go, what he might do?'' he asked, though he doubted she had any more information to give him.

She hesitated for so long that he almost hung up the phone. Then she finally continued. "He...he spoke about wanting to kill Lissa and her new husband—and even that friend of Lissa's who had talked her into leaving him.''

The premonition that had driven Travis to make his phone calls finally had a justification. "Was the friend's name Jenny?''

"Yes, yes. That was it. And Mr. Hunter, you have to understand, I never believed Ted would ever do the things he threatened to.''

"You were wrong.''

He broke the connection, too angry and apprehensive to offer anyone absolution. Lissa's death might have been prevented if Shafer's mother had made one phone call to the police. It was too late to save Lissa, but he was determined that she would be the last one who died by Shafer's hand.

Travis knew that the one shot he'd been able to get off had wounded the gunman in the mall. Shafer could have been using the past six weeks to recuperate, just as he, himself, had. Now Shafer could be ready to strike again, this time with Jenny as his target.

Chewing his lip impatiently, Travis dialed the number to Rob's ranch and waited. He counted twenty rings before finally giving up.

His last call was to the Layton City sheriff's office. He quickly explained the situation to Sheriff Dawson and asked the lawman to drive out and warn Jenny.

Travis replaced the receiver and looked down at the rose he held clutched in one hand. Andrea and Bonnie were still at Landon Ranch. If Shafer decided to strike now...

As he turned and ran for the gate, he realized just how much he cared for both of them. He just hoped that realization hadn't come too late.

Chapter Ten

"...Right, Andrea?"

Andrea looked at Jenny blankly. "Excuse me?"

The other woman gave her an indulgent smile that made Andrea wonder how many times she had already repeated her question. "I was saying that it's nice to be able to just sit back and be an observer once in a while."

Andrea looked at the new litter of kittens that the Landon Ranch barn cat had just delivered without any help from the resident vet. She tried to return Jenny's smile, but she couldn't quite manage it.

Jenny pulled her into a brief, comforting hug. "Then again, sometimes it's the hardest thing in the world to just watch and wait, isn't it?"

"Yes." Especially when she knew that no matter how things turned out, Travis wouldn't be coming back to her. She wondered if he would even keep the promise she had pried out of him and send the rose.

Somehow, she doubted it, but she had told both Jenny and Maggie to be on the lookout for it, just in case.

She had learned to accept his death once, but how did one learn to bear waiting when she knew the wait would go on forever? But, then, she had already learned the answer to that. One day at a time. One hour at a time. One minute at a time.

And this time around she wasn't alone. Cuddling Bonnie closer to her chest, she made an effort to share Jenny's enthusiasm. "The kittens really are cute. When I was a little girl, I..."

The sound of a car engine approaching made her heart lurch to her throat, and her words faded away in midsentence. When she turned toward the open barn door and saw the sheriff's car pull up outside, she began to pray.

She rushed toward the doorway, but before she could reach it, Sheriff Dawson had already walked inside.

"Good afternoon, ladies," the big man said, touching the brim of his Stetson. "I was wondering why I couldn't get y'all on the phone."

Jenny stepped forward to meet him. "Maggie and her kids are in the house, but they just went in a minute ago. Why were you trying to reach us?"

"Travis Hunter called me from Chicago and said he'd be back here in a couple of hours."

If Andrea hadn't been holding the baby, she was sure her knees would have buckled. She took a deep breath and willed herself to concentrate. It couldn't be true! What had happened with Valente? Maybe she had heard wrong, maybe... But what the sheriff was saying now seemed to confirm it. Travis was alive and he was coming home!

"Travis sent me out to check on you," Dawson continued. "He seems to think that Ted Shafer was the one who shot him and Lissa down in San Antone."

"Isn't that Lissa's ex-husband?" Andrea asked, trying to make sense of it all.

"Yes," Jenny confirmed with a confused frown. "But it couldn't have been him. He's still in prison!"

"He was paroled, then he disappeared around the time of the shooting. He's probably long gone by now, but it seems he made some threats against you, Miz Emory. So it's best to take some precautions until he's apprehended. Where are the rest of your people right now?"

Andrea watched, concerned, as Jenny rubbed her palms against the legs of her jeans. "Our dude-ranch guests have left—no more are due until next week. My cook has the day off, and Rob went to help Jude with a repair over at the Double Diamond. Andrea and I are alone here with Maggie and the children."

The sheriff nodded. "Okay, then. Y'all stay in the house and keep the doors locked, just in case. I'll stick around out here until the men get back."

"That's kind of you, Sheriff."

"No problem. I—"

There was a muffled, *popping* sound that made Andrea jump. She watched in astonishment as the sheriff stopped talking and slumped to the floor at her feet.

Jenny started to kneel down beside him.

"Back away from him, Jenny, or this nice lady here is going to join him."

Andrea looked up to see a tall, slender man in an army fatigue jacket enter the barn. But she still didn't grasp what was happening until she saw the gun in his hand. A gun that was pointed at her.

A cold fear gripped her. Fear for herself, her friends, and most of all for the baby she held in her arms.

"Jenny, darlin', he's beyond help. And you should know by now that Ted Shafer doesn't make idle threats."

Jenny, her face dead white, straightened up and moved away from Sheriff Dawson.

Shafer stepped closer, grinning ear to ear. "Say thank you, Jenny. That bullet was meant to be yours. But now that I know Travis Hunter is on his way here, I think I'll do things a little differently. I'll just have you drive the sheriff's car inside the barn, then we'll go into the house and wait for Hunter together."

Jenny licked her lips. "I...I thought I was the one you came for, Ted. Why don't you lock my friend here in the barn and take my Jeep? You could take me along as a hostage in case something goes wrong, and we could be in Mexico in no time. If you wait around until Travis gets back, you're going to lose your chance to get away."

Shafer gave a dry, appreciative chuckle. "You haven't changed, have you, Jenny? You still like to tell people what they ought to do. Just like you told Lissa she ought to leave me."

His smile disappeared. "It just so happens that I'm not concerned with getting away. The only thing I have to go on living for right now is revenge. And

I'm gonna get every last drop of that revenge before I die.''

He took a step closer, his dark eyes narrowed, their expression ugly. ''Lissa wouldn't have a baby for me. Did you know that? Well, I got even with her. I killed her and her baby, and now I'm gonna get the man she let father it.''

If Andrea had felt fear before, what she felt now was pure terror. What would this man do if he found out that Lissa's baby had survived?

Shafer jerked his head in the direction of the door. ''Now get that car in here, Jenny, so we can go on up to the house. And remember, you may have nothing to lose, but if you make one wrong move, your friend here is going to pay the price.''

Andrea watched numbly as Jenny complied, her thoughts racing. What would happen when Travis arrived? Would he somehow be able to save them, or would he be walking into a death trap?

For the second time that day, she realized there was only one thing she could do. Wait.

''I don't believe this!''

Travis's fist hit the top of Mike's desk, nearly upsetting the cup of coffee the other man had just poured.

Manelli lifted a client's file out of his chair and sat down across from Travis. ''What?''

''The sheriff's office hasn't heard from Sheriff Dawson in over three hours, and the phone at the ranch is out of order. But that idiot, Deputy Jones, seems to think Dawson's just inside the house, having lunch and 'watching over the ladies.'''

"It's a possibility," Mike said, after a second's hesitation. "Just because Shafer's loose out there somewhere doesn't mean he's going to pick today to go after Jenny."

Intellectually, Travis knew that. But the feeling of impending doom that had lain coiled inside his chest for hours now told him differently. He pushed to his feet. "I'm going out to the ranch."

Mike stood up and reached for his jacket, but Travis shook his head. "I need you to stay here at the agency and keep trying to locate Shafer—in case I guessed wrong."

Manelli tossed a look over his shoulder at the other two investigators who were already on their phones, carrying out those same instructions. Then he looked back at his boss. But Travis was already on his way to the door.

"I work better alone, Mike."

"Yeah," Mike muttered at the closing door. "Well, someday, boss, you're gonna wish you'd had me there to back you up."

"What if he doesn't come?"

Shafer looked at Andrea across the dining room table. "He'll come."

"What if his plane crashed, or his car ran out of gas, or he simply changed his mind?"

Grinning, Shafer waggled the gun at her like an admonishing finger. "You, darlin', are a pessimist."

Andrea opened her mouth to pursue the matter further, but a warning look from Jenny stopped her from speaking. She closed her eyes and willed herself to relax. What was wrong with her, anyway? Was she trying to provoke Shafer?

But she knew what was wrong. They had been sitting around the dining room table for over three hours now. Sitting in silence with the tension and the terror that Shafer had brought with him into what had once been a peaceful refuge. Every moment had become an eternity, and Andrea was beginning to think even death would be preferable to suffering through much more of this.

She looked up, glancing at Maggie on her right and Jenny on her left. She wondered what they were thinking. Of ways to overpower Shafer? Jenny would be, certainly. Jenny knew what Shafer had in store for her, once Travis arrived. But even Jenny didn't dare to make a move against him. None of them did. Shafer had seen to that.

Her gaze turned back to him, and she had to fight to keep her expression neutral, to keep the hatred from showing.

He sat in his dining room chair with all the confidence of a king on his throne, a baby carrier on the floor on each side of him, and Todd on his lap.

Maggie's little boy had long since responded to the overwhelming fear and the boredom in the way of children. He had escaped into sleep. Andrea only wished that she had felt free to do the same.

"You don't like waiting, do you, lady?"

Andrea's gaze riveted on Shafer's. "No, I don't. But you seem to."

"Oh, I don't like it. I'm just used to it. You learn to wait in prison. You learn to wait or you go crazy."

Andrea straightened in her chair, giving Shafer a defiant look that seemed to amuse him even more. Not long ago, she had prayed for Travis's return. Now she prayed that he would never come. She made her bargain with God. She would sit here and face Shafer for all eternity. Just let Travis stay away.

Travis left the car he'd rented at the airport half a mile from the ranch house and walked the rest of the way.

When he came to the small graveyard overlooking the house, he began to move stealthily, using the outbuildings, the corral and an old wagon to hide his approach.

He circled around to the back of the house, wondering where Sheriff Dawson's car was, wondering what its absence signified. He wished it were night instead of a sun-bright afternoon. But he was afraid to wait for darkness to fall. If Shafer was in there, every minute might count.

Pausing at the window of the back bedroom that belonged to Rob and Jenny, he used a sliver of space between two panels of drapery to peer inside. As he had expected, the room was empty. He eased the window open and climbed over the ledge.

Gun drawn, he crept down the hall, checking out each room he passed. It occurred to him that he was going to feel pretty foolish if nothing was amiss and he came upon Andrea or Jenny and scared them half to death. But right now he would have welcomed the feeling of humiliation that meant he'd guessed wrong. The oppressive silence in a house that had always been so full of noise and life was stretching his nerves to the breaking point.

Approaching the end of the hallway, he saw that the living room was empty—and that the dining room was not. He had only a partial view of one chair—enough to send an icy bolt of fear shooting through him.

He recognized the army fatigue jacket and the face from his nightmares. Shafer was sitting there in a position that commanded a view of both the front and the kitchen doors—and a peripheral view of the hallway Travis was standing in. And he had the baby carriers at his side and Todd in his arms. He also held a .38 in his right hand, presumably pointing at another hostage.

The gun didn't scare Travis a tenth as much as the proximity of the children did. There was no way he would risk a shot. No way in hell. And if he tried to get close enough to take Shafer out any other way, the bastard would see him coming and nail him before he'd moved a foot.

Travis leaned back against the wall, chewing on his lip and silently cursing his own stubbornness. Mike had been right. He should have brought backup along. What he needed right now was a diversion, something that would get Shafer to look away from the hallway.

Then it occurred to Travis that he did have a potential source of help. The other people who had to be seated at the dining room table. The Emorys—who, or how many, he had no way of telling. Maybe even the sheriff, though he doubted Shafer would have left Dawson alive. And Andrea.

The thought of Andrea seated at that table and Bonnie in one of those baby carriers was enough to paralyze him with fear, if he let it. And if he let it, there would be no one to help them. Ruthlessly, he pushed the fear aside.

Shafer had already killed once, so he had nothing left to lose. Travis didn't know why the man had restrained himself this long. But he did know that, any minute now, Shafer could decide to open fire on his hostages.

What Travis needed was some way to let the people at the table know that he was here. He thought about it for a minute before he hit on an idea. It might not work at all, but maybe, if he got lucky…

Andrea almost cried out in alarm when she felt the hand squeeze her knee. Then she realized that it had to have been Maggie. She looked toward the other woman in surprise.

Since Shafer had entered the house, the vibrant, laughing Maggie that Andrea had come to know had transformed herself into a silent, all-but-invisible shadow.

Even Shafer, who had described himself as a "walking dead man," had seemed to come back to life when he'd first seen Jenny's beautiful sister-in-law. He'd hardly been able to take his eyes off of her, and he'd made comments that had caused Andrea to cringe. Maggie had wilted under his lustful attentions, withdrawing into herself until even Shafer had become bored with trying to draw her out.

Now Andrea wondered what it was that had caused Maggie to come out of her self-imposed isolation. She raised an eyebrow, silently asking the other woman what she wanted.

Maggie looked straight ahead, toward the hallway, then her gaze dropped to the tabletop again.

After allowing several seconds to pass, Andrea casually turned her head to the left, as though stretching her neck. On the floor, just at the entrance to the hallway, lay a single red rose.

Andrea felt a soaring exhilaration that was immediately followed by crushing fear. Travis was here! He was here and now Shafer had the opportunity to kill him.

Fighting to control her fear, Andrea tried to think how she could help her husband. Where, exactly, was he? The rose was at the entrance to the hallway....

Suddenly, Andrea knew what Travis wanted. She had to find a way to divert Shafer's attention from the hallway so that Travis could approach him from that direction. But how? If she tried anything too obvious, Shafer would catch on.

Then she looked at Maggie and thought of an idea. It wasn't an idea she liked, but it might be one that worked.

"Maggie, isn't it time to feed Karyn?" she asked, trying to sound as matter-of-fact as she could.

She felt Jenny's quizzical stare boring into her from one side and saw Maggie's mouth gape open slightly. Twin flags of pink appeared, marking the blond woman's high cheekbones.

Andrea continued to look at Maggie, willing her to understand. And knew the moment that she did. Knew by the hurt in her eyes, by the resignation in the sudden slump of her shoulders. Silently, Andrea begged her friend's forgiveness.

"Wait a minute," Shafer said, finally roused. He looked back and forth between them. "The kid's not even crying! What is this?"

There was a moment of silence that seemed to stretch out for an hour. Then Maggie said softly, "It's important to keep on a regular schedule with this kind of thing."

With a resolute toss of her head, Maggie bent down and lifted her daughter out of the carrier and into her arms. Then, slowly, she began to unfasten the buttons on her high-necked blouse.

Shafer's eyes widened, then fastened on the blond woman like a magnet.

Saying a silent prayer, Travis glided out of the hallway and into the living room.

Andrea tensed, forcing herself not to look in his direction. Instead, she grabbed Jenny's hand beneath the table, trying to alert her friend, whose back was to the hallway, that something was about to happen.

Travis was halfway to his goal, and Andrea was already anticipating the victory, when Bonnie began to cry.

Shafer instinctively turned his head toward the sound and looked directly at Travis.

"Stop!"

Travis froze as Shafer's gun swung away from Andrea, leveled at him, and then dipped down toward the baby carrier where Bonnie lay.

"Everyone just stop right where they are. And you,

Hunter. You drop whatever that is you got in your hand.'' He watched as the cloth Travis held fell to the floor. ''What the hell is that?''

''Chloroform,'' Travis said, his mind searching frantically for a way out, but not finding any.

''Chloroform?'' Shafer echoed. ''Oh, you play rough, Hunter! You wouldn't happen to have anything a little, uh, stronger on you, would you?''

Moving slowly, Travis pulled out his gun.

''Throw it that way,'' Shafer told him, indicating the other end of the living room.

Travis did as he was told. The gun hit the far wall and fell to the floor.

''Is that it?'' Shafer asked, his finger visibly tightening on the trigger of his own weapon.

A whimpering sound tore its way out of Andrea's throat.

Travis swallowed hard and nodded. ''That's it.''

''Good. Because it's taken me six weeks to get over the last bullet you pumped into me.'' Shafer grinned and looked at Travis with every evidence of satisfaction. ''But you're not such a big man now, huh?''

Then he glanced down at Bonnie, apparently angered that his moment of triumph was being upstaged by her crying. ''Somebody shut this kid up before I do!''

Jenny, who was sitting within reach of the baby, plucked Bonnie from her carrier, and the infant immediately quieted.

Shafer let the gun move up to cover Andrea again, his gaze still on Travis. ''When I got out of prison, I tracked you and Lissa to San Antonio. I picked a mall for the shooting because it was easier for me to blend in with the crowd and get close to you. After I got over that bullet wound you gave me, I tried to find you again, but your landlord said you went to England. So I came after Jenny here, instead. Then I heard you were coming, too, so I decided to wait for you."

"I'm flattered."

"You ought to be."

Travis sought out Andrea's gaze, trying to say goodbye. When Shafer finished talking, the man was going to start shooting. And as soon as that gun was pointed his way, he would make his move. If he got lucky, maybe he could take Shafer with him.

Andrea gathered herself, planning on making her move before Shafer had a chance to turn the gun on Travis again. If she was fast enough, she might buy her husband the time to reach Shafer and disarm him.

She looked up at the man she loved, hating the fact she had found him only to lose him again. They'd had so little time together, and they'd wasted most of it quarreling and hurting each other.

And Bonnie...

"You should have stayed away from my wife, Hunter."

Andrea saw the gun begin to move toward Travis.

"No!" She threw herself across the table, grabbing for Shafer's arm. Then everything seemed to happen at once.

Shafer released Todd so he could use two arms to grapple with her. Maggie and Jenny dived for the floor, taking the children with them. Shafer's gun went off, blasting a hole in the ceiling and causing a hail-storm of plaster.

Andrea felt Shafer wrench his arm free of her grasp just as Travis tackled the man. Both men rolled to the floor, still struggling for possession of Shafer's gun.

Coughing and covered with plaster dust, Andrea ran across the living room and retrieved Travis's gun. It felt heavy and alien in her hands. But, for once, she didn't fear it. It was the man who had invaded her home that she feared, the man who threatened her husband and her baby. She held the gun at arm's length and pointed it in the direction of the two men rolling at her feet.

"Give Travis your gun, Shafer! Give him your gun, now!"

Shafer continued to struggle.

"Do as I say or I swear I'll pull this trigger!"

"You...think...I...care?" Shafer panted, his gaze shifting to hers for an instant.

Grunting with the effort, Travis used the opportunity to deliver a blow that sent pulsations of agony through his bad shoulder and finally dislodged the gun from Shafer's hand.

Using his old police handcuffs, Travis cuffed the dazed man and pocketed the gun. Then he looked up to see that Andrea still had his gun leveled at Shafer. The expression in her eyes made his blood run cold.

"No!" He moved to get up, to go to her, but Shafer writhed under him, and he had to lean heavily on the smaller man to subdue him.

Andrea's hand began to tremble visibly. She hesitated for an endless second. Then there were the sounds of doors bursting open, men shouting. The strange spell that had held her in its grip was broken. She lowered the gun, and it slipped from her suddenly numb fingers onto the floor.

Chapter Eleven

"Andrea, are you all right?"

Blinking, Andrea looked at Jenny and nodded. She pushed aside the memory of what had just happened to her. She had to deal with it, and she would. But not now. Now she had more important things to do.

Carefully, very carefully, she reached out and took a snuffling, clearly upset Bonnie into her arms. Unwrapping the baby, she examined her quickly, but thoroughly, reassuring herself that all was well. Then she hugged her daughter close against her heart, gradually becoming aware of what was going on around her.

She saw Rob set the large revolver he'd been carrying down on the dining room table and pull Jenny into his arms for a fervent kiss. "I was so afraid, Jen!" she heard him whisper. "I don't know what I'd do if anything happened to you." Jenny beamed and held him, her life back on its even course now that Rob was there to anchor it.

Still holding a wailing Karyn and clutching a bewildered, sleepy-eyed Todd by the hand, Maggie threw herself into Jude's arms. Jude leaned his rifle against a chair and closed those big arms around his wife like an impenetrable shield.

For the first time Andrea understood how much strength and confidence Maggie drew from the love of the homely, taciturn man she had married. Andrea watched as Jude indicated Shafer with a jerk of his head. "Did he touch you?" he asked his wife in a soft voice.

Maggie burrowed deeper into her husband's embrace and shook her head.

Jude pinned Shafer with a glare that finally caught the other man's attention. Shafer stopped struggling against Travis's hold. Wide-eyed, he looked up at Jude's scarred countenance as if he'd suddenly seen the gates of hell swing open in front of him and heard the devil offer him a guided tour.

After a long moment, Jude nodded to the deputy who was standing by. "In that case, I guess I'll let you have him."

Shafer lurched to his feet, stumbling in his haste to let Deputy Jones lead him out of the house.

Then Andrea felt hands on her shoulders and turned to find herself in Travis's arms. She smiled up at him.

Travis ran his hands over her face, brushing away bits of plaster, confirming to himself that she was unharmed. He started to tell her all the things he'd vowed to tell her if he survived the afternoon. But he'd barely finished explaining what had happened with Valente, when Bonnie began to cry again.

"Is she okay?" Travis asked anxiously, his hand stroking the baby's soft hair.

"Just hungry," Andrea assured him.

She took the baby into the kitchen to heat up a bottle, and Travis turned to talk to Rob.

Andrea didn't see her husband again until Bonnie was asleep in her crib, and she was able to sit down at the kitchen table with Travis and the Emorys for dinner.

By then, she had had time to come up with a worry that she could hardly force herself to acknowledge. Travis had married her when he'd been sure he was either going to die or disappear. Now that he was back, would he want to live with her as man and wife, or would he want to end the marriage of convenience he'd entered into so hastily?

Andrea sat through the dinner, picking at her food and forcing herself to listen as Jude and Rob told their side of the day's events. Alerted by a call from Mike Manelli, they'd been returning to Landon Ranch when they'd come across Travis's car parked half a mile away from the ranch house. Finding nothing wrong with the car, they'd become even more suspicious and decided to approach the house on foot.

Rob took up the story as he scooped the last spoonful of potato salad from the serving bowl onto his plate. "When we discovered the sheriff in the barn, it was pretty clear to us that Manelli's warning had been right on target. I used the radio in the sheriff's car to call for help."

His food forgotten, Rob looked at Jenny, his eyes dark with the memory. "We weren't sure where Travis was or what was going on in the house, and we were afraid that Deputy Jones wouldn't arrive in time. So I took the sheriff's gun and Jude got his rifle. But when we stole a look through the kitchen window and saw Shafer in the dining room holding Todd and that gun, we didn't know what the hell to do. So we waited. Then we heard a gunshot, and we could see Andrea fighting with Shafer, so we came on in. The deputy finally got here a minute later."

"Is Sheriff Dawson going to be all right?" Maggie asked, spooning some green beans onto Todd's plate despite his halfhearted protests.

"I called his office a little while ago," Jenny told her. "The helicopter got him to the hospital in San Antonio okay, and the doctors there are saying he'll be fine. The bullet glanced off his skull instead of penetrating. It knocked him unconscious, and it was a nasty-looking wound, so Shafer assumed he was dead."

"Cool!" Todd exclaimed, draining his milk glass.

His mother gave him a quelling glance—and a hug. "Eat your vegetables!"

"It'll take more than a bullet to kill ol' Dawson," Jude said confidently, spearing up a forkful of beef. "That man has always had the hardest head of anyone I know."

Rob gave his older brother a devilish grin. "Present company excepted, of course."

A soft, healing wave of laughter rippled around the

table, and Andrea forced a smile. But she couldn't help looking at Travis and wondering what the rest of this too-eventful day had in store for her.

"Come take a ride with me. I want to talk to you."

Andrea almost dropped the bowl she was carrying to the kitchen when she heard Travis's whispered suggestion. "I've got to help with the dinner dishes," she told him, trying to delay the inevitable.

Then Maggie walked by, taking away the bowl and her excuse. "You go ahead, Andrea. Jenny will be back in here in a minute. She and I can manage."

Untying her apron, Andrea gave up the fight. "All right, Travis, but give me a minute, okay? I'll meet you at the car."

When her husband had closed the kitchen door behind him, Andrea walked over to where Maggie was filling the sink with water.

"About the suggestion I made for distracting Shafer earlier... Well, I just want to apologize. I—"

Maggie turned toward her, her forehead creased by a frown. "Don't you dare be sorry! It was a smart idea, and it almost worked."

"I never meant to hurt you," Andrea felt compelled to add.

"I know," Maggie said. "That's why it's okay."

They embraced, and Andrea stepped outside feeling good about the resolution she'd reached with Maggie. If only the situation with Travis were as simple!

Andrea found Travis leaning against Rob's pickup. It was parked in front of the barn and the sight of that familiar structure brought back memories of what had happened there only a few hours before. Would she ever be able to look at the building again without remembering?

"Thinking about Shafer?" Travis asked, pushing away from the truck and opening the passenger-side door for her.

Andrea pressed her lips together and nodded. She started to get into the vehicle, then hesitated. "Do you think he'll get what he deserves?"

"With me as an eyewitness to Lissa's murder, and you and Jenny able to testify to what happened to Sheriff Dawson—not to mention the rest of it—I doubt Shafer will ever be back to bother us again."

He watched Andrea climb into the truck and saw that she was still wearing the same distracted look he'd been noticing for hours. As they began rolling down the driveway, he asked softly, "Do you want to talk about what happened today?"

Andrea thought about it and decided that she did. "I've been afraid of guns all my life, Travis. Today I realized why. When I was holding that gun on Shafer, I wanted to use it. He'd killed Lissa and almost killed Bonnie before she'd even had a chance to be born. Then he'd come back and threatened her again. Her, you, and good people—people who had offered me shelter and friendship. I wanted him never to be able to come back and hurt any of us again. I felt like I was..." She stopped speaking, searching for the words.

Travis glanced at her as he turned the steering wheel and headed across an open pasture that his rental car could never have traversed. "You felt like—what's that phrase?—judge, jury and executioner all rolled into one?''

''No,'' Andrea said, turning to look at him. ''I felt like God. All-powerful. Able to decide whether Shafer deserved to live or die. No one, *no one* should have the right to buy that power for the price of a gun.''

One corner of Travis's mouth curved up. ''I respect your feelings,'' he told her. ''But you'll forgive me if I don't hang up my gun just yet. There are a lot of really bad guys out there like our friend, Shafer, whose ideals aren't quite so high. They don't mind playing God, and I don't mind admitting that they scare me.''

Andrea had been anticipating that response. ''You'll forgive me if *I* don't agree with you. I'm going to do everything I can to see that gun control becomes a reality in this country so that people like Shafer can't get their hands on a gun to begin with.''

''Even run for office?''

That was one comment she hadn't expected to hear from him. But once she'd rolled the idea around in her mind, she decided she liked it. ''Maybe.''

''Well, you've certainly got the money and the connections for a career in politics.''

Andrea tensed. She hadn't detected any sarcasm in Travis's comment, but his remark reminded her of the animosity that had always existed between them, his hostility toward her social class and all that it represented.

Suddenly, she realized that she was still being a coward, still afraid to confront her problems with Travis head-on. If a parting with him was inevitable, then let it not be as it had been the first time, shrouded by pain and deception. Let it be clean and honest, and hurt them both as little as possible.

"Pretty, isn't it?"

Becoming aware that the truck was no longer in motion, Andrea looked around her. In the fast-fading light, she saw that they were sitting at the bottom of a hill, in an open grassy area surrounded by trees. It was a lovely site, but she had other things on her mind.

Gathering her courage, she turned in her seat to face Travis. "I just want you to know that I won't try to keep you if you don't want to stay. But I hope that we can make some kind of an arrangement as far as Bonnie is concerned. I know—"

"You said you loved me!" Travis's exclamation cut into her words and her thoughts. She looked at the bewildered expression on his face and felt a surge of something that resembled hope.

Travis's own hopes had plummeted to his feet. "Have you changed your mind now that I came back?"

Andrea searched his eyes for the answer she so desperately needed to discover. "No, I haven't changed my mind, but I thought you might have changed yours."

Travis slowly released the breath he'd been holding. "No way!"

He leaned toward her and pulled her closer. Then he gave her the kiss she'd been so much in need of since he'd returned. She wanted to give herself up to it, but a part of her felt a twinge of hurt and disappointment. He still hadn't said that he loved her. But at least he wanted them to stay together, to be a family.

She told herself that that was the important thing. And who knew what the future might bring?

Travis pulled away slightly and looked into her eyes. "I'm not quite sure what that kiss meant. Are you willing to try marriage with me again, or not?"

Andrea put her head against his shoulder, wanting to believe that a future with Travis was possible. "I think we were both to blame for what happened the first time around. This time, if we remember to talk to each other, try our best to communicate, then I think we can make it work. After all, we're older and a little wiser now."

Sliding his fingers into her hair and holding her close, Travis grinned. "Older, anyway." Then his expression became more serious as he asked her the question that had been worrying him the most. "Where are we going to live?"

Andrea pulled back and blinked up at him, astonished that that point hadn't even occurred to her until now. She thought about it and realized that she'd already made up her mind.

What did she really have in Chicago? An expensive condominium that was beautifully furnished, but empty of any voice save her own. Parents and a long list of acquaintances she felt only the most superficial connection to. And a teaching career that had been her whole life up until about two weeks ago. But things had changed for her in those two short weeks. Now she had a family and friends who she loved and who loved her in return.

"Since you work in San Antonio, we can live there," she told him. "But I'd like to keep the house in Layton City. Maybe we could make it out here for some weekends and holidays. I want Bonnie to grow up knowing the Emorys.''

Travis leaned back against the door of the truck, one arm across the steering wheel and one resting on the back of the seat. He stared at her, unable to absorb what she'd just said. ''But what about your work?''

''I'm going to finish my thesis and get my Ph.D. But, after that, my career can be put on hold for a while. Bonnie can't. I waited a long time to have a child. I want to be with her and watch her grow.''

Smiling, Travis took her hand. ''This morning, I decided the same thing. I know you used to worry about the danger involved in police work, and being a private detective isn't exactly the ideal job for a family man. Mike Manelli's been after me to let him buy the agency, and Rob offered to sell me some land. What would you think of being married to a rancher and living in a house right up there?''

Andrea looked past him at the grass-covered hill and realized why he had brought her out here. ''I think I'd love it,'' she told him sincerely. But she would have traded every foot of this land and lived in a tent if she could have heard him say ''I love you.''

Telling herself to count her blessings, she gave him a smile and a lingering kiss.

Travis pulled away with a groan. ''We'd better stop this, before it goes too far. The front seat of a pickup isn't exactly the best place to make love.''

''Oh, really?'' Andrea said, doing her best to look stern. ''Am I in the company of an expert on that subject?''

"Former expert," Travis assured her. "C'mon, let me show you the view."

Hand in hand, they climbed up to the top of the hill together. Andrea strained to see in the fast-gathering darkness, and what she saw was beautiful to her eyes. Rolling grassland, trees, and, in the distance, a blue creek meandering on its way. She had always lived among the larger-than-life granite towers of Chicago and felt at home. But this area called to a different part of her soul, a part that craved serenity and peace. The part that loved a man called Travis Hunter.

"By the way," she said, looking up at him with a smile, "Am I Mrs. Hunter or Mrs. Morgan?"

"You mean, am I going to take back my old name now that things are straightened out with Valente?"

Shifting his view from the darkening distances to his wife, Travis put his arms around her and drew her close. "I've thought about it. But since Trey Morgan is officially dead and all my papers—birth certificate, social security card and a brand-new marriage license—are all in the name of Travis Hunter, I'll continue to be Travis Hunter."

He took her face in both hands and looked at her intently. "In my heart, that's who I am. A new man. And you and I will be starting a new life together."

He was bending to kiss her when Andrea put one finger to his lips to hold him off. She wanted to accept the wonderful things he was saying and believe in the new life he was talking about, but she could feel the doubt eating away at her contentment. And she knew it would continue to do so until she brought that doubt into the open.

"I have to know, Travis. You're not just staying with me for Bonnie's sake, are you? Or because of some misplaced pity or guilt about my hysterectomy?"

Travis's smile disappeared, and he felt anger and frustration replace the joy that had filled him to overflowing only seconds before. What was wrong with the woman, anyway? Didn't she know how he felt about her? Then he realized what was wrong, and his anger faded.

"Have I told you lately just how much I love you, Mrs. Hunter?"

Andrea was afraid to believe what she was hearing. "But you said—"

"Yeah, I said a lot of stupid things. But the truth is, I love you. I never stopped loving you. I was just too angry and too hurt by the divorce to admit it to you or to myself. I realized how I felt about you when I was in Chicago and found out that Shafer was on the loose and that you might be in danger. I just forgot to tell you. But I'm going to try real hard to make up for the delay."

He gave her a kiss that erased her last doubt. Cloaked by friendly darkness, they sank onto the soft grass.

Travis was on fire for her, body and soul. He pushed aside her clothes, paying little attention to buttons or zippers, finding and pleasuring all the secret places of her body with his hands and tongue.

Andrea touched him in turn, burrowing under his shirt to run her hands over the muscles of his chest and unzipping his jeans to caress the hard, velvet length of him with her fingers and her mouth.

Unable to hold back any longer, Travis rolled onto his back and lifted her above him. Slowly, she eased her body down onto his, making him a part of her once more. Then she began to move, and Travis had to bite his lip hard to keep from exploding.

Still undulating against him, she leaned forward and sealed their union with a kiss. "I love you," she whispered.

Travis was beyond speech. He returned her kiss, arching up into her, grasping her hips as she pulled away, then came back to him.

He moved one hand across the smooth expanse of her belly, then dropped it lower, seeking and finding the key to her pleasure. His other hand moved up to caress the aching tip of one breast.

Andrea felt the delicious tension building inside her. Then it crested and broke. Shuddering in ecstasy, she let one hand drop down behind her to caress the heavy roundness between his thighs.

With a wordless exclamation, Travis turned over, placing her beneath him. He drove into her until her aftershocks of pleasure became true pleasure once more. Then he stiffened in her arms as his own climax consumed him.

In the aftermath, Andrea held him tightly, vowing never to let him go again.

Travis moved to his side, bringing her with him, searching her features in the moonlight. "I love you, too, Andi," he said, still fighting to catch his breath. "I love you, too."

Andrea had no doubt that he meant every word. She knew that this time it would work out between them. They had been given a rare second chance, and they would make the most of it.

They would build a house on this hill, raise Bonnie in it and grow old there together, surrounded by their friends: Maggie, who had the joy of knowing that Jude loved and respected her for the person she was and not for the way she looked; Jenny and her Rob, the man who had loved her enough to go through anything to claim her.

Yes, here Andrea knew she would have true friends, the warm family she had always wanted, and all the love she would ever need.

Her hopes and dreams had died with Trey Morgan, only to be resurrected with Travis Hunter. There had been pain along the way, but as she held her husband in her arms, she knew that it had all been worth it. She had rediscovered a love too strong and too true to die. A love that would sustain her for the rest of her life.

*   *   *   *   *

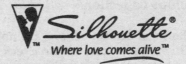

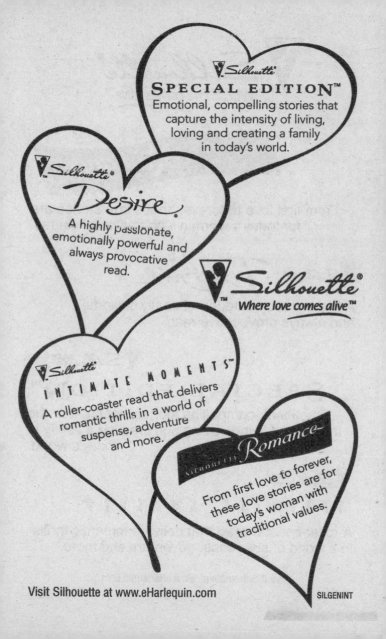

Where love comes alive™

From first love to forever, these love stories are
for today's woman with traditional values.

A highly passionate, emotionally powerful
and always provocative read.

SPECIAL EDITION™

Emotional, compelling stories that capture the
intensity of living, loving and creating a family in
today's world.

INTIMATE MOMENTS™

A roller-coaster read that delivers romantic thrills
in a world of suspense, adventure and more.

Visit Silhouette at www.eHarlequin.com

SDIR2